Small Claims

Small Claims

ANDREW KAUFMAN

Invisible Publishing
Halifax & Picton

Library and Archives Canada Cataloguing in Publication

Kaufman, Andrew, 1968-, author
    Small claims / Andrew Kaufman.

Issued in print and electronic formats.
ISBN 978-1-926743-90-5 (softcover).--ISBN 978-1-926743-95-0 (EPUB)

    I. Title.

PS8571.A892S63 2017   C813'.6   C2017-901241-X
                                              C2017-901242-8

Edited by Stephanie Domet
Cover and interior design by Megan Fildes | Typeset in Laurentian
With thanks to type designer Rod McDonald

Printed and bound in Canada

Invisible Publishing | Halifax & Picton
www.invisiblepublishing.com

We acknowledge the support of the Canada Council for the Arts which last year invested $20.1 million in writing and publishing throughout Canada.

Canada Council   Conseil des Arts
for the Arts   du Canada

For Marlo

No one can flatter himself that he is immune to the spirit of his own epoch, or even that he possesses a full understanding of it.

— Carl Jung

Three cans of water provokes me.

— Sloan

PART THREE | LIONIZED

PART ONE

DEFENDANTS & PLAINTIFFS

01. THE BICYCLE INCIDENT

It is difficult to tell whether this trial has just finished or will soon begin. The defendant, Mac, is a tall man with a barrel chest who leans against a long wooden table on the left, gigantic and alone. To his right, behind an identical wooden table, is the plaintiff, Ted, who wears a bright red golf shirt that seems wholly inappropriate. He sits beside his lawyer, who types on a Blackberry with both of her thumbs. Up on the dais, the justice and the court reporter talk in whispers. The windowless courtroom is overlit by eighteen fluorescent tubes, and there's a clock mounted high on the east wall. Both the clock and the lights hum.

"Listen, why don't I just call my lawyer again?" Mac keeps his wall-like mass still as he tentatively lifts his massive hands toward the fluorescent lighting. He seems unfamiliar with embarrassment, unsure what body language will most effectively express it. The light bounces off his head, which is bald except for two tufts of salt-and-pepper hair that stick out at the sides like a bull's horns.

The court reporter swivels in his chair. He looks up at Justice Olivetti, who nods her head.

"What's his number?"

"Four one six..." Mac says. There are twelve other people watching this trial, but I'm the only one who's amazed that Mac can recite his lawyer's phone number from memory.

I am here in courtroom 313 for two reasons: I got lost on the way to getting my street parking permit renewed, and this morning I found myself running down the middle of Shaw, chasing a bicyclist, wanting to kill him. The moments immediately preceding my chasing of the bicyclist were extremely peaceful. I was walking my kids to school, which is the only significant act in life that I perform with daily repetition. It is the closest thing I have to a ritual. Jack is nine. Jenny is seven. The three of us leave the house together shortly after 8:35. About half a block later Jack takes off, runs as fast as he can, and rounds the corner long before Jenny and I get there. This is how he declares his independence.

The next four or five seconds are the most important in my day. It is during this time that Jenny is most likely to take my hand. She has recently begun expressing her independence as well, and her method of displaying self-sufficiency is refusing to hold her father's hand. If I try to hold hers, she'll pull it away. Jenny only takes my hand when she forgets she isn't doing that anymore, and the most likely time for this to happen is just after Jack has rounded the corner and disappeared from sight.

Jenny didn't reach for my hand this morning, but I was okay with that. I'm grateful for the mornings she does. I know the number of times she will take my hand is now finite, that at some point in the next handful of years she'll stop doing it altogether, or at least so infrequently that it will feel surprising when she does. I know that in her late twenties she'll start holding my hand again, but by then it'll be different: she'll be holding my hand to give me support, not to gain it from me.

"I'd like to go swimming," she told me, her empty hands dangling at the ends of her sleeves.

"Swimming? That could be arranged. Maybe on the weekend."

"No, today. Instead of school. Jack wants to, too. We talked about it."

"It's a school day. We have to get to school!"

It is these simple requests that overwhelm me. Why is my

response to always say no, to disagree, to shut things down? How badly do I need to feel more powerful than an eight-year-old? Why don't I just take them swimming? Certainly a day, or even just the morning spent in the pool, would develop their bodies and their minds more effectively than sitting at a desk, paying moderate attention to their teachers. I feel like I would be a much better person if I could become the kind of dad who throws homework on the fire and takes the kids to some fabulous thing instead, to be the kind of dad who teaches them how to get the most out of life. But I never do, and trying to figure out why I don't was preoccupying me as we rounded the corner at Shaw, the only busy street we have to cross to get to their school. I looked up just in time to see my son step into the road without looking, while a thin, fashionable twentysomething on a vintage bicycle barrelled through the stop sign toward him.

"It's going straight to voice mail," the court reporter says.

Mac shrugs his shoulders, which makes the skin at the back of his neck wrinkle into three distinct lines. He looks over his shoulder. He raises his arms and lowers them again. None of this succeeds in producing his attorney. Justice Olivetti exhales. Her breath ripples the bangs of her silver hair. She doesn't try to hide her frustration. This session is part four of a trial that began in August. Today is Monday, September 10. The conflict in question originated three years ago.

"This is what we're going to do." Justice Olivetti shakes open her glasses and puts them on her nose. "The trial will continue sir, with or without your lawyer. We are going to finish the proceedings today. So, I will ask you—and I will ask you to respect me and this court with a truthful answer—do you have any more testimony?"

Mac pulls in a large breath, filling his lungs in the manner of a swimmer about to attempt a long underwater swim. He's about to speak when Justice Olivetti gives him a look that is both maternal and hostile.

"Any *relevant* testimony?"

The clock hums. The plaintiff looks up from his professionally manicured fingernails. His lawyer's thumbs fall still. Justice Olivetti stares her stony stare, and Mac allows the lungful of air to escape.

"No. I guess not. That's pretty much all that happened."

"You'll have to take the stand so your cross-examination can begin."

Mac nods, takes the stand, and gets sworn in. There is no chair on the stand, so Mac is forced to remain standing. He makes fists of his meaty hands, rests them on top of the witness stand's railing, and leans forward. Pushing shallow breaths through his nose, Mac tilts back his head until his chin is pointing directly at Ted the plaintiff. He continues staring at Ted with angry eyes, and it becomes easy to imagine a large golden ring through Mac's nose and cartoon bursts of steam coming out of his nostrils—Mac the Minotaur.

After being sworn in, Mac remains silent, allowing his posture to speak for him. The angle of his shoulders, the slits of his eyes, the tight grip of his fingers around the wooden railing of the witness stand—all these mannerisms work together, expressing with undeniable clarity that Mac thinks this trial is squandering precious moments of his precious life, that simply being here is a slight unto his noble nature. Mac's arrogance and put-upon impatience reminds me of someone. It takes several moments before I realize that someone is me.

Jack didn't know what to do. He froze. I froze, too. They were too far away from me to do anything. The bicyclist sped directly toward my son. The sole concession he made was to steer slightly to the right, allowing him to carve out a space, roughly the shape and size of a canoe, around my son.

This is where a blank spot starts, about six seconds that my subconscious has redacted, the time between realizing that the bicyclist wasn't going to stop and hearing my dress shoes smack against the asphalt as I ran down the middle of Shaw Street, screaming after him. I do not know what happened to me during these moments, what thoughts and decisions were conducted in my head that the rest of my mind doesn't want me to remember. But I do know this—as I came to, when the thick black marker of self-censorship was lifted, I wasn't running after the bicyclist simply because he'd endangered my son, or from the fear that I'd already held Jack's hand for the last time, but because I envied his confidence, his cavalier attitude, the degree to which he was so certain that life was going to work out for him.

These qualities made me despise the bicyclist, kept me running after him like the archetypal angry farm dog on the lonely side road of middle age, long after it became obvious that I wasn't going to catch him. I ran for another three or four seconds. I became winded. I stopped in the middle of the street, hands on my knees, desperately trying to get my breath back. Eventually, I walked back to my children, who stared at me, amazed but disturbed, realizing for the very first time that they actually had no idea who their father really is.

We walked to school. No one talked. Jenny did not hold my hand. Then, I went to work, which I do in a small, well-lit room at the back of our house. I write industrial manuals for a living. If you've ever bought anything from the Howlstein Corporation, including their subsidiaries Wanton Electronics and Quizz Appliances, you've read my work. I wrote until noon. I didn't get a lot done, and it didn't feel like I was going to, so I drove to the City of Toronto Municipal and Judicial Building at 47 Sheppard Avenue East. I needed to get my street-parking pass renewed, and the deadline to do it through the Internet had passed. Now, the only way I could get a properly dated sticker and avoid nightly parking tickets was to go all the way to North York, pay twenty dollars to park, then stand in line at the permits office located on the third floor, room 389. This infuriates me. Why make it so difficult? Why have only one office that the entire city of Toronto has to bottleneck through between the hours of noon and four, Tuesday, Wednesday, and Thursday? I know that much of my anger is misdirected, that I'm really mad at myself for missing the deadline: that, once again, my lack of organization has put me at a disadvantage. I am a wet dog shaking myself dry, flinging not water but anger into the world. I find myself shouting profanities at other drivers from behind the wheel of my car, struggling not to scream when people in front of me insist on using exact change, or when mechanical voices on the telephone ask me to hold.

There was a time, not that long ago, when I would have done nothing but hug Jack after the bicycle incident, been overjoyed that he was unscathed. I would have cut the bicyclist some slack, understood that he was rushing, wasn't thinking, just a kid. I would have remembered the numerous times I've been that bicyclist myself. I would have been able to leave it at that. Sometime during the last two or three years, my generally optimistic perspective slowly devolved, and I've become a cranky, bitter curmudgeon. I have reached a state of empathy fatigue. My optimism has been drained, a car battery forced to keep the headlights illuminated with the engine off and the radio on, as my id and superego grope like teenagers in the back seat, oblivious to the damage their negligence is causing.

But within me there's a strong desire to recapture my empathetic nature. And that desire resonated, practically pushed me inside the room, when I happened past the open door of courtroom 313. The triptych of plaintiff, defendant, adjudicator, all with their own well-defined roles to play, all three working within a structure that promised a clear outcome, a straightforward determinate resolution, was irresistible. I sat down on an uncomfortable wooden bench amongst the future plaintiffs and defendants, and once I began watching the proceedings, I couldn't look away. What I saw was an entire branch of our juridical system working so hard for such tiny stakes. I may have come into courtroom 313 because I'd failed to navigate this minotaur's domain of hallways and strangely non-sequential room numbers, but I stayed because I need to believe I'm redeemable, that we're all redeemable. I continued sitting there in the hopes of witnessing something noble enough to smash the cynicism that time and failure and sadness have encased around my heart.

Mac's lawyer still has not arrived. Ted's golf shirt continues to shine its red glare of disrespect. His counsel, Sandra, a thin young woman in a grey pantsuit and sensibly high heels, puts the unpainted nails of her thumb and index finger to the bridge of her nose and squeezes. It's easy to see Sandra as a sapling, young and green. Her hair is two weeks in need of a cut. Her right leg only ceases bouncing as she stands up. But there is a hushed confidence, a mostly masked, self-assured authority revealed by the confidence in her fingers as she opens one of the six binders stacked neatly to her right, flips pages, and looks up at Mac.

"So. Mr. Minto. You're very experienced in sourcing products from China for Canadians?"

"Yes."

"Salad bowls? Cellphones?"

"More so on the electronics, yes."

"You have a strong relationship with China? With Chinese manufacturers?"

"Yes?" Mac tilts his head slightly to the right. You can almost hear him evaluating Sandra's worth, wondering if she's more powerful than she appears, if her questions are, perhaps, leading him into some kind of trap, a labyrinth constructed of facts. But Mac's doubt is not as strong as his arrogance, and he pushes these thoughts away. For the next fifteen minutes, Sandra asks a series of questions that appear to establish nothing but facts. She gets Mac to agree that in September of 2009 he was hired by Ted's company, Waffles! Waffles! Waffles! as a subcontractor. That Mac agreed to travel to China, where he would design and source a waffle maker that met specific technical requirements needed by the Waffles! Waffles! Waffles! franchise. That once the prototype was approved, he would oversee production of 220 units. That he was given a lot of money to accomplish this: $50,125.

"You were paid $3,000 for consulting, $4,500 for costs, $6,000 for travel to China. As well, a $10,000 deposit to a factory in China." Sandra doesn't ask this as a question, but she remains silent long enough that Mac treats it as one.

"That's all right. Correct," he says.

"That leaves $26,625 unaccounted for. Where are these funds, Mr. Minto?"

"I don't have the funds."

"Where are they?"

"In China."

"Where in China?"

"The factory!"

"Did you submit documentation to this effect?"

"No."

"Why didn't you provide documents to the court today?"

"It's in Chinese. Can you read Chinese?"

"Is it at your lawyer's office? Your lawyer who isn't here?"

"I haven't provided any documentation."

"So you never told the court about it?"

"I was never asked to do so."

"You never told?"

"I was never *asked*!"

"You misplaced the documentation?"

"I have no documents."

"None at all?"

"That's not how they do things over there."

"No packing slips? No tracking numbers? No emails?"

"I have nothing here."

"So there is something somewhere? Some documentation? A paper trail of some kind?"

"I don't have it."

"Where is it?"

"In China!" Mac stares at Sandra and huffs, his blunt thoughts about her easy to read.

"I'm going to ask you straight, Mr. Minto. There never was a prototype, was there?"

Mac corrects his posture, stands up straight, take a breath. He tilts back his head and looks down defiantly at Sandra, at all of us, at the very idea that this court has any right to cast judgment upon him. Mac has failed to convince even his own lawyer to show up, he's presented a shockingly small amount of evidence to prove his innocence, while Sandra has done an excellent job of establishing his guilt—yet he continues projecting outrage at being suspect.

What I want to see is Mac throw up his hands and yell at the top of his lungs that he took the money. I would also accept him claiming to have spent the missing $26,625 bribing Chinese officials. Even a rant, apologetic or otherwise, about the woman he met in a bar and the favours he bought from her, would redeem Mac in my eyes. Any of these responses would fundamentally alter how I see Mac and, I suspect, how he sees himself. As he stands there, silent, motionless, trying to decide how to answer Sandra's question, there is something in Mac's expression, a sadness, maybe even shame, that speaks of the potential for nobility. Some part of Mac is aware that this moment is an opportunity, the kind life rarely presents, to wipe the slate clean, to start again, to become the man he's always suspected lives deep inside him. But it's not to be.

"That's not correct!" Mr. Minto says.

"Really? Are you sure about that?" Sandra flips a tab in her binder, her fingers finding a passage like a butcher sharpening a knife. Mac's upper body slumps forward, his meaty hands grip the sides of the witness stand. His eyes turn from slits to ovals as he realizes what he's done, that he's lost his only way out, that now he's trapped inside the labyrinth forever.

02. PLAINTIFFS & DEFENDANTS

Courtroom 347 has yellow walls, no windows, and a power couple in their mid-forties sitting next—but not close—to each other behind the long wooden table on the right. The defendants have arrived before the bailiff, the court reporter, and the justice. Even the plaintiffs haven't arrived yet. The garbage cans are empty. The long wooden tables smell of lemon-scented cleaner. The carpet has been vacuumed so recently that the lines left by the machine are still visible, rake marks in a zen garden of dry beige berber. The defendants continue staring straight ahead. They do not touch. Whether this absence of physical contact is the result of respecting each other's personal space or the fear of reprisal should they breach that personal space is unclear, although that absence is what convinces me they're husband and wife.

"We're on the wrong side." Helen has jet-black hair and she's at least fifteen pounds too thin, which gives her prominent cheekbones a touch of Halloween. Her husband shakes his head with a condescending certainty. His charcoal suit is gorgeous, professionally tailored, which, combined with the sense of entitlement he somehow manages to project solely through the sharp angle of his shoulders, informs the world that this is a man used to making decisions, not mistakes. This may or may not explain why he fails to believe his wife, even though there's a sign less than six inches in front of him that reads *Plaintiff*.

"Are you sure?"

Helen has already collected her binders and pens. She moves to the table on the left, opens a binder, and begins making notes with a silver ballpoint pen. She pushes the pen forcefully into the paper. It's easy to imagine that Helen isn't composing preparatory notes but simply writing the phrase *I hate my husband* over and over again. And if she were holding a knife and not a pen, she'd be carving this phrase into the table.

Last night, my wife, Julie, and I went to the restaurant where we usually go to celebrate things. It had been quite some time since we'd been there, so long that the interior had been redecorated since our last visit. We didn't recognize any of the staff. We didn't get the table by the window and were seated in a booth by the kitchen. I sat across from Julie. I crossed my legs. I didn't open my menu because I was going to have what I always have. When I looked up at Julie, I got the distinct impression she was using all of her self-control to resist picking up her fork and gleefully, joyfully, repeatedly stabbing it into my hand.

"Aren't you hungry?" she asked.

"Very. I'm very hungry."

"What are you having?"

"The peppercorn steak."

"I don't see it."

"What?"

"It's not here."

"Really?"

"No, I'm lying to you." Julie put down her menu, quickly. This created a breeze strong enough to make the candle on the table flicker, although it wasn't enough to extinguish the flame altogether. Julie didn't notice. She wasn't looking at the candle. She looked directly at me for the first time since we'd sat down. Her eyes were narrow. The skin around her mouth was tight.

Seeing how angry she was hurt me, which I attempted

to cover up by becoming angry myself. So that's how we stayed for a while, sitting across the table from each other, not speaking, just being angry.

I wasn't planning on going to small claims court today. It's a surprise that I'm here. I'm not sure when I made the decision to come, or if I made it at all. This morning, after walking Jenny and Jack to school, I decided to take a stroll away from my house instead of toward it. This is something I sometimes do, part of preparing to write, a meditative exercise to help me focus. Five minutes later, I found myself standing in front of the Christie subway entrance. I already felt like a passenger. I paid the fare, took the Bloor train east, and transferred to the Yonge line, which I rode north to the North York stop. A flight of stairs, a push through the turnstile, a short walk, and I found myself standing in front 47 Sheppard Avenue East.

The building is a grey concrete rectangle squinting into the street through narrow linear windows. It stands as a physical manifestation of governmental wishy-washiness, a design so obviously chosen by committee, green-lit specifically because it was deemed the least offensive option. I'm just guessing, of course, but how else would a building like this get built? Who else but those eager to be re-elected, to rock no boats, willing to please none over displeasing a few, would have given this concrete shitbox the honour of housing the noblest aspects of our civilization? My gaze kept slipping off it, choosing instead to focus on a small bank of clouds to the right, which drifted across the sky like a group of lost children.

Just to the right of the elevator on the third floor is a sheet of green paper stapled to a corkboard. It lists the dockets of various courtrooms. I chose courtroom 347 partly at random and partly because there were several people waiting in the hallway outside it and I knew I could file in with everyone else unnoticed. That's how I came to be here. How Helen and Doug arrived is a little more complicated. They still haven't made eye contact. All three of us sit quietly, staring at nothing for five minutes, until Anthony, a man ten percent too young, wearing a suit twenty percent too fashionable, arrives.

Anthony stands behind the table on the right, opens a vintage-style leather briefcase, then looks over at Ted and Helen. He gives a small, sincere wave. Neither Ted nor Helen returns it. Anthony looks a bit hurt by the snub. Then Justice Royal enters the courtroom and everyone rises. Justice Royal is a tall, thin man with an afro of curly white hair that gives his head the impression of being a dandelion gone to seed. Without fanfare or fidgeting, without any sense of ritual at all, Justice Royal sits down.

"Okay, over to you." Justice Royal points at Doug, and the trial begins.

"I'll just be fifteen minutes." Doug collects a stack of papers. He takes a deep breath, holds it dramatically, then slowly exhales. Glasses hang around his neck, and Doug leaves them there as he begins reading from a prepared statement. His cadence is both monotonous and stumbling, a perfect, potentially rehearsed impression of an eight-year-old narrator. Five minutes into his prepared statement, Helen begins studying her right palm, running her left thumb up and down the various lines. The fifteen-minute mark comes and goes. Time stops being literal, as the monotony of Doug's voice stretches each second longer and longer. Twenty-seven minutes later, Justice Royal interrupts.

"Is this still your opening statement?"

"It is."

"Is there more?" Justice Royal turns in his chair to look over his shoulder at the clock behind him.

"Yes."

"A lot more?"

"I'll be brief."

"Very well."

Doug looks down at his papers and resumes reading, his nasally narration strangely in sync with the overlit space. Helen no longer looks directly in front of her. She's looking to the right, her eyes cast as far away from the sight of her husband as the room allows.

We ordered. The food came. We ate the food. Just after the dishes were cleared and we'd both refused dessert, Julie took the white linen napkin off her lap, folded it neatly, and set it aside. That feeling of insecurity returned, the one I've been having more and more, an unshakable certainty that the next ten or twelve seconds could witness the end of my marriage.

Neither of us can figure out exactly what the problem is or how to stop the fighting, or the arguing, or the constant undercutting of every decision the other makes, even the small ones. We know that we still love each other, but we've started to wonder if our love is too strong to die or if we're too weak to kill it. It is not a comfortable feeling, this notion that holding on to love, fighting for it, spending so much of our time and energy, complicating our lives to defend it, may not be born of a noble instinct but of weakness.

"Why are you so angry all the time?" Julie asked, her voice quiet and calm. Her face became clocklike, an instrument objectively stating not the time but that all of this, our unhappiness, the conflict between us, the pale dark pall that's been cast over the future, is my fault. Perhaps it is. Maybe I am solely to blame. But I'm afraid to even contemplate this for fear that admitting it would transform me, make me someone else, an imitation of myself, a scarecrow stuffed with mildewed hay, slumping beneath the large black ravens circling overhead. It's difficult to explain. The importance of maintaining this rigidly feels much more honourable and valid in my head, as if inflexibility is the only thing keeping my masculinity from deflating completely.

Julie continued staring at me, her expression expressing nothing, articulating neither anger nor contempt, but containing no compassion or love either. The need to hear my response to her question hung in the air between us, a cheap special effect from a black-and-white movie, a hovering spectre only the two of us could see. I found myself leaning forward in my chair, anxious to hear what I was going to say just as much as Julie, if not slightly more.

Doug continues talking. We learn that he and Helen own a 6,000-square-foot, one-hundred-year-old home worth approximately $3.5 million in downtown Toronto. In 2010, they decided to renovate the kitchen. For reasons that Doug fails to make clear, their regular bank—the bank that holds the mortgage to their seven-bedroom, four-bathroom dream home in the affluent and coveted Rosedale neighbourhood—was unwilling to give them a new mortgage. Doug and Helen were asking for $175,000, a sum that does not seem outrageous considering the potential resale price of their home in the ludicrously hot Toronto housing market.

Although not willing to cough up the funds themselves, their bank was more than happy to recommend an interested third party, a loan company named Perpetual. Doug concedes that a draft mortgage was drawn up, but he maintains that this agreement was never signed. This is very important to him. He repeats it several times, so I will, too: the draft contract was never signed.

Now, it's September, and even though Doug hasn't signed his name at the bottom of the drafted mortgage with the Perpetual Loan Company, using a cursive that I can only speculate would be flowery and ornate, the type of signature that prioritizes dramatic loops and swirls over legibility—a signature much like my own—work on the renovation somehow gets underway. Doug never explicitly states this, but I'm assuming that the couple used their own money—or worse, family money—as stopgap financing to hire a contractor and begin the renovation. Anxious to pay his bills, Doug's now eager to sign and get the money, but Perpetual has begun demanding to see things, trivial things, like building permits.

Perpetual sees these demands as satisfying legal requirements. Doug is of the opinion that these building permits fall outside the scope of the project and are nothing but an attempt to sandbag him and his wife, that the paperwork is unnecessary and designed to rack up fees and expenses. This difference in opinion leads to an impasse. Doug receives no money. The deal goes into limbo, like sea monkeys stuck in their packaging, and the entire transaction is trapped in suspended animation until December 31, New Year's Eve.

Maybe Helen was putting the finishing touches on her makeup and wiggling into a little black dress as Doug fiddled with sterling-silver cufflinks. Perhaps she was rushed, as the hired car had already arrived to take them both to a chic downtown party. Whatever the circumstances, this is when Helen emailed Perpetual and broke it off, informed them that the couple would no longer be requiring their services. Now we've reached the present. The kitchen renovation is almost done and Perpetual is suing Doug and Helen for commitment, legal, and standby fees incurred, a figure they reckon to be $11,397. It seems important to note that this case is being fought over money that never changed hands.

The only answer I could come up with to give Julie, to explain why I'm perpetually angry, a response to justify or at least articulate why a dark cynical tar coats each and every one of my emotions, was the story of how our daughter puked all over my back last January. It was just the three of us—me, Jenny, and Jack—in the car. I'm not sure why Julie wasn't there. I was rushing because we were running late, driving east on the 401 to their ski lesson. Jenny's vomiting was truly inspired. She used to get carsick all the time, but I thought she'd grown out of it. The vomit sprayed onto the back of my neck with considerable force. Thick and warm, it dripped downward between my shirt and my skin. I took shallow breaths through my mouth and tried not to think about the chunky cubes bathed in hot mucus slime soaking my shirt. Beginning to gag, I rolled down the window and looked for an exit. It was snowing. There was a thin layer of slush under the tires. To my left, a white rental van travelled a little faster than we were. On my right was the eighteen-wheeler I was attempting to pass. My daughter started to cry. I tried to change lanes, but the transport blocked my way and we missed the first exit.

"It smells! It smells so bad!" Jack screamed.

"It's okay."

"But she stinks!"

"It's okay!"

"She smells so bad!"

"Stop it!"

"So bad!"

"Goddamn it! Just be a good brother!" I screamed at my son. He began to cry. They were both crying. I wanted to cry, too. The white rental van sped up. His back right tire kicked spray onto my windshield and at the same moment he began to move into my lane. To the right were the middle six wheels of the transport truck. I was terrified and desperately trying to hide this fact from my children.

"I'm sorry, I shouldn't have yelled! I'm sorry!"

My daughter's puke slid farther down my back. It cooled and stuck to my skin. The van was directly in front of me. Its tail lights came on. I applied my brakes. Our car began to fishtail. Not a lot, but enough. The transport zoomed by me, revealing the next exit. Without looking in my rear-view mirror, I pulled into the right-hand lane.

"How's your sister?"

"I'm sorry!"

"I'm sorry, too!"

Decelerating, I took the turnoff, then twisted the rear-view mirror so I could see her. Puke coated her ski jacket, her car seat, her hair. I forced a smile that I hoped expressed benevolence. Jenny puked again, the vomit seeping out of her mouth like a pot of vegetable soup boiling over on the stove. I turned the mirror so I couldn't see her anymore and pulled into a gas station.

The amount of cleanup I was able to perform with the scratchy brown paper towels dispensed at the pumps was minimal. Much of the puke was matted into Jenny's hair and rubbing it with the paper towels only made it worse. The stench of vomit mixed with the smell of gasoline. Gagging, I handed my phone to my son, and his vomit-coated sister was quickly forgotten as he began playing Minecraft. I hate the power those games have over him.

"I still feel sick," Jenny said.

"I'll be right back."

Jack didn't look up from my phone. Jenny looked at me like she expected I was never coming back. The inside of the gas station was designed to induce the sensation of an operating room, overlit with white walls, glistening stainless-steel shelves holding products arranged in calculated rows. I walked to the counter, behind which a teenager pretended not to notice me, the only customer he had. I admit that I stared too long at his black fingernail polish.

"Can I get some water?"

"In the cooler, at the back." He shook his shaggy head in the general direction, leaving his hands free to continue holding his phone.

"No, sorry, my daughter threw up in the car. I just need some water to clean her up."

"Bottles of water are in the cooler."

"Are you serious?"

He shrugged.

"Come on."

He shrugged again.

"Really?"

"I can't just give you water."

"Yes. You can. You easily can."

"You'll have to buy a bottle."

"Of water? You can't even give me water?"

"Sorry."

"Then give me the key to the bathroom."

"Bathrooms are for customers."

If I were forced to pinpoint the exact moment in which I lost faith in this world, it wouldn't be in grade school, when I was taught about Nazis and death camps and that the only two times the world has ever banded together was to fight each other. It wouldn't be our currently suspended disbelief, having discovered global warming and yet continuing to do nothing about it. It wouldn't be my first trip to the big city, when I saw scruffy men sleeping outdoors. It wouldn't be during Grade Ten, when my mother sat me down and told me that my father was having an affair and that all of our lives, as we knew them, were ending. The precise second that the world finally, once and for all, irredeemably failed to live up to my expectations was as I walked to the cooler at the back of that gas-station convenience store. Surveying the prices, I selected the cheapest bottle and carried it back to the counter. The cashier punched buttons into the cash register. The screen told me I owed $1.47. I put a toonie on the counter and he gave me back fifty cents.

"Now give me the key to the bathroom."

It was a small victory. Taking it made me a small man. This is the problem with the modern world: even the victories diminish you. Leaving the bottle of water behind, I took the key and helped my daughter out of the car. She held my hand as we walked to the bathroom.

"I can't go into the boys."

"It's an emergency."

Inside the tiny room, I removed the mess from my

daughter and spread it around the bathroom. Flecks were flicked on the sink, the mirror, the wall. The smell of vomit inhabited the space in a way I knew would not soon leave. The garbage can overflowed with paper towels grown soggy with water and puke. When my daughter was vomit-free, or at least as vomit-free as the circumstances allowed, I took her hand and opened the bathroom door.

"What about the mess?"

I said nothing. I ushered my daughter back to our car. My son still didn't look up as I strapped Jenny into her car seat beside him. I lowered all four windows and drove to the ski hill. The kids had their lesson. It was only on the way home, as I saw the gas station from the other side of the 401, that I realized the key to the bathroom was still in my pocket.

With waiters hovering nearby, wanting us to leave so they could reset the table, Julie waited for my answer, but I couldn't tell her the story of Jenny puking. Given the fragile state of our intimacies, the justifiable doubt she has in the nature of my character, it would be too easy for her to mis-interpret the story as just another rant about how I carry the heavy burden of dealing with our children. Or, even worse, she could have easily taken the side of the kid behind the counter, reprimanded me for leaving the poor clerk with such a mess, for setting such a bad example for our children, a perspective that would only have started another fight.

But even more threatening to me, more intimidating than her neutral stare, provoking more anxiety than the idea of getting a lawyer and putting the house up for sale, the real reason I didn't present the story of Jenny's puke and the trip to the gas-station bathroom was that the telling would have made me vulnerable. And I have lost the ability to be vulnerable around my wife, which seems, to me at least, to be the entire point of being married to someone.

"What is it that you want?" I said instead.

"That's it? That's your answer?"

"Do you even know?"

"I want someone who makes their own decisions," she responded, quickly. "I want someone who can stand on their own. I've already got children. I don't need you to be one. I want...I want a man of action."

It's was her final phrase, so cliché, so black and white, so Bogart and Bacall, that froze me, that made me unable to reply. It cast its severe and damning power over me because I knew it was true. I didn't admit this, either. I just shrugged. I put on my coat and so did she and we walked out of the restaurant single file, both of us with our hands thrust firmly and deeply into our pockets.

Doug's hands stay silently at his side, moving only when he needs to flips a page. His statement continues, rambling, for seventeen more minutes, twelve of which are spent presenting his original arguments in various uninspired and repetitious ways. Finally, he concludes.

"Okay," Justice Royal sighs. "Would you like to call your first witness?"

"That's all I've prepared."

"All right." Justice Royal turns his attention to Anthony, counsel for the plaintiff. "Would you like to cross?"

"Yup." Anthony bounces out of his chair and stands at attention. He stretches his arms over his head, commits a small bow toward Justice Royal, and then takes a single piece of paper from a manila folder. He sets the paper in the middle of the table and places his pointer finger underneath the first printed line of text.

"You acknowledge that you had an agreement with Perpetual?"

"Um…"

"Do you?"

"It was unsigned."

"Do you acknowledge the existence of this agreement?"

"I do."

And it goes from there. Anthony works down his list of questions, rhetorically swinging from branch to branch, point to point, emotionless, egoless, a perfect extension of the faceless corporation he represents. Doug's not used to being challenged and his dislike for Anthony makes him appear defensive. Or maybe he just is defensive. Whatever the cause, the effect isn't flattering. During his opening statement, Doug was bewilderingly incompetent to an almost lovable degree—now he's coming off as evasive and elitist. Even though I've grown to hate Doug in a very short time, and I'm fully aware that I'm projecting each and every aspect of myself that I currently dislike onto him—my wishy-washiness, my inept earning of money, my inability to keep track of dates, my failure to appreciate my wife—I find myself feeling sorry for the guy. This is the degree to which Doug's getting pummelled.

"Would the building permits we requested have increased or decreased your property value?"

"That would require an assessment."

"Okay. Would the renovations to your house have increased the value of your home?"

"Perhaps?"

"Substantially?"

"Possibly."

"And property taxes are based on a home's value. Correct?"

"Yes."

"So then it's safe to say that the building permits we requested would have increased your property value?"

"That is a possibility."

"Did you resist getting the building permits in order for the city to remain unaware of the increase in your property's value?"

"No. I did not. Absolutely not."

Anthony turns the piece of paper over. There is only one question written on the other side. Helen looks up from her note-taking and glances at her husband. The look she gives him is not filled with love. The courtroom is quiet. For a moment I think that Anthony won't ask any more questions, that he's happy with how much shit he's already kicked out of Doug. But this is not the case. Anthony has one more question. If anything in life is guaranteed, it's that there will always be one more question, and it's the one that'll bring you down.

"Did you get the building permits?"

"Excuse me?"

"Have you gone ahead with these renovations?" For the first time Anthony's voice is not neutral but strong, filled with suspicion and contempt. Doug's pause is long. The radiators come on with a metallic tick loud enough to drown out the hum of the electric clock.

"The necessary building permits were acquired," Doug says.

"How many?"

"Several."

"Of the seven building permits Perpetual asked you to acquire, how many did you eventually acquire?"

"I'm not sure of the exact number."

"I have the documentation right here."

"Okay."

"Seven. You applied for and received seven building permits. Does that seem right to you?"

"Yes."

"Thank you. No further questions."

Anthony nods, clicks his pen, sits down. He's trying very hard not to smile, which is the only act of charity I will ever see him perform.

Doug looks at his wife. Helen stares, intensely, at something invisible and very far away. Doug leaves the witness stand. He sits beside her. When he leans toward her, she leans away.

"Are you done, then?" Justice Royal asks.

"Yes. I think we are," Helen says.

03. FORGIVE US OUR ECCENTRICITIES AS WE FORGIVE THE ECCENTRICITIES OF OTHERS: PART ONE

Another possible source of my anger and frustration, something to explain why my optimism is no longer strong enough to sustain belief in the limited eighteen-month warranty for the Quizz #2-17 Performa Vacuum, why everything tastes bland and flavourless, and why nothing excites me, is that my fourth novel, the one that was supposed to reinvigorate my flagging literary career, is terrible. It's simply bad. I'm not exaggerating or being my own worst critic. As a work of fiction, the book undeniably fails to come together. I have published three novels and certainly there have been sections within these published pages that I feel failed to express my talents fully, swaths of twenty to thirty consecutive pages that were certainly not written from the top of my game—but never have I felt this way about an entire book.

This is the first time I've deemed an entire manuscript unpublishable. I know, without doubt, that the defects and deficiencies of this novel cannot be redeemed by vigorous editing, a reimagining of plot, or a deeper understanding of the characters' needs and desires. This is not just a novel that needs work: this is a novel that doesn't work. It's just fucking bad. I know this in my heart to be true, and that has never happened to me before.

That being said, there are some really good moments in it. I think it starts off well. This is the opening paragraph...

> I'm not going to say exactly what I was running from. It was the same thing you are. Different numbers in the same equation, that's all:

x (chases) y = y (runs). Maybe you don't even realize you have an x. You should find that very frightening, because it means your x is so big and terrifying you can't even find the nerve to look over your shoulder. So steel your courage and search your heart and ask yourself what your x is.

Is it the lover you've fallen out of love with, but can't seem to leave? The best friend you abandoned in their moment of need? Perhaps it's just the undeniable knowledge that grabs you by the throat late at night and shakes you awake, screams silently in your head how somewhere along the line you made the wrong decision and now the life you're living is a complete and utter lie.

We all have an x. So it doesn't matter what my x was, even though mine caused me to stand on the gravel shoulder of the southbound lanes of the Don Valley Parkway trying to hitch a ride to anywhere else.

Not bad, eh? The novel goes completely to shit very shortly, two or three pages after that. The book is weird, but the weirdness is forced, not allegorical or metaphorical or fabulist, but just weird for weird's sake. The story follows Simon, a man in his late twenties who was born with green skin, webbed hands, and webbed feet. Doesn't that sound marketable? In a literary landscape ruled by realism, where no book with a fantastical premise has even been shortlisted for a major award—and don't give me that shit about Ishiguro's *Never Let Me Go*, because that's simply the exception that proves the rule—I have no fucking idea why I thought, why I was so stubbornly and absolutely convinced, that a character who's little more than a giant talking frog would resonate with readers.

But that's not the worst of it. The book quickly turns into a surrealistic coming-of-age story, a narrative format and arc that work together in much the same way that bicycle tires and glass do. The plot, such as it is, follows Simon, the talking frog, who was raised by his human mother and who never met his father, as he sets off to find himself and, hopefully, others like him. I think it was an attempt to stand out, to gain recognition through originality rather than artistic merit, the literary equivalent of a gimmick. This ultimately led to the creation a sort of semantic new wave band, turning me into a CanLit version of A Flock of Seagulls or Men Without Hats, but without all the sales and cool haircuts.

Two years ago, when I started *Forgive Us Our Eccentricities as We Forgive the Eccentricities of Others*, I thought it was going to be my breakthrough. But the novel's simply unreadable and, even worse, boring. It's not just me who thinks this. My best friend Zach, who's been the first reader for all of my books, thinks it stinks.

I wish I had the strength to burn it. I am so aware of how bad this book is that I can even see the rare passages, the three successful paragraphs tucked amongst twenty pages of shit, where it's not. I think the third chapter ends well. Our green-skinned Kerouac starts hitchhiking, but near the end of his third day he still hasn't made it out of Ontario. Of course, his failure is the result of him having green skin, although this is never explicitly stated in the text. Why? Because I believed it would be more literary not to do so, as if being obscure was a narrative virtue.

It's afternoon when a car pulls over for him. Simon runs

up to the tinted passenger window and it lowers: there is a green-skinned man behind the wheel. Can you believe it? Same webbed hands, hairless head, the whole bit. The other giant talking frog, the one driving a fucking Buick Electra, offers Simon a ride. For hours they drive north in silence. Once again, I choose to leave the character's motivation for this silence "open." Simon remains in the passenger seat, heading east on the Trans-Canada Highway when...

The driver suddenly took the first exit we passed. It was 7:15 in the evening and the sun was three inches from the horizon, spilling bottles of orange and yellow paint. There was a high ridge of hills to our right, but he didn't drive toward them. We passed a gas station and he pulled in, drove around to the back, and parked the car pointing at a brick wall, the front bumper less than six inches from it.

Apprehension and fear filled me—here I was sitting in a stranger's car, nobody knew where I was, and I didn't even know this man's name. I had put my trust in him simply because his skin was green. As these undeniable realities struck me, I turned my whole body, picked up my knapsack with my left hand, and found the door handle with my right.

"Go if you have to," he said. Both of his hands returned to the steering wheel and he stared out the front windshield at the brick wall. "But it might be worth it just to sit here, quietly, for the next several minutes before you do. All I'm asking you to do is sit here and watch the sun set."

There was something about his voice, calm but serious, that made me pause. Although I kept my hand on the door handle and my knapsack on my lap, I stayed in the passenger seat. I stared ahead, thought I'd give it a try, matched my breathing with his. I did everything just like he was doing. I just didn't get it. Once he'd mentioned the sunset, I'd assumed he would restart the car, find a different location, at the very least reverse so that he wasn't parked directly behind the back wall of a gas station. When I looked through the front windshield, all I saw, all it was possible to see, was a brick wall. "I can't even see the sun," I said.

"Who said you had to see the sun to watch it set?"

I stared ahead, unblinkingly, and after three or four minutes I began to see how the light changed, and the colours with it. I watched the red brick turn to rust, and then to an almost-brown before it became a dark, dark red. I saw the dashboard turn purplish-blue and then to coal. My own skin turned more shades of green than I had ever seen before. Every second that passed brought out a new colour to my skin, each one so rich, so deep, it seemed like it should have had its own name, not just be considered a shade of something else.

"Wow," I said.

"There ya go." He breathed out a breath I hadn't noticed he'd been holding. "You're gonna be fine. You're gonna be just fine. My name is Ást."

"Simon."

We shook hands, our mutual webbing making this awkward in a most endearing way. Ást turned on the headlights, started the engine, backed away from the wall, and returned to the highway.

I think that one of the reasons *Forgive Us Our Eccentricities as We Forgive the Eccentricities of Others* is such a total and ultimate disaster is that it was written from a place of wishful thinking, a novel that wasn't a story I needed to tell, but a collection of pages with words on them sequenced to impress. Even this scene, which is honestly one of the best in the book, is a minor observation, something that could have been distilled to a throwaway comment by a minor character. It would actually have been stronger, created a greater impact on the reader, if it had been presented within the narrative as a minor turn, something that allowed the reader to discover a small piece of wisdom on their own terms, instead of me shoving it in their face like some oversized phallus in a bit of poorly lit pornography. As it is, the only comfort I can take from *Forgive Us Our Eccentricities As We Forgive the Eccentricities of Others* is that, as failures go, it is a spectacular one.

This is small comfort and does little to quell my fears that I've lost it, that I will never write another piece of worthwhile prose in my life, that the very thing that used to make me feel safe and secure has been taken from me, like a beloved stuffed animal pulled from the arms of a toddler in a well-meaning but unwise effort to prepare him for the first day of school.

"Where's your evidehhhhhhnce?"

The plaintiff's attorney, Conrad, joyfully lingers on the final syllable, filling the room with a long, guttural roll. His grey hair is pulled into a tight, tiny ponytail. His glasses are half frames, which he constantly looks over, and the diamond in his ear sits near the bottom of a fleshy, unattached lobe. I do not like him. He's a blowhard, a show-off, the kind of man buoyed through the construction of elitism, who sustains an artificially elevated sense of self-worth by pretending to love jazz and sending back perfectly cooked steaks in restaurants.

"We need to see the evidehhhhhhnce!"

"It's my word against his. My word against his!" The defendant, Tony, is a big guy wearing a fine black suit and a wrinkled white shirt. A narrow band of untanned skin is visible on the ring finger of his left hand. Tony waves in the general direction of the plaintiff. He's been on the stand for thirty minutes and responded to at least that many questions. His voice has become high and thin over the course of this cross-examination. The problem is that all of Tony's answers, each and every one of them, lack specifics. He has placed words in such a sequence that they resemble answers, but ultimately lack the spine of empirical evidence. Tony's dancing around something, most likely the truth, and the effort of this performance is tuckering him out. He rests his forearms on the wooden railing of the witness box, curving his torso and hunching his shoulders until his body takes the shape of a question mark.

"No forms? No emails? No records of recommendaaations?"

"I'm not going to waste the court's time with boxes of paper." Tony raises his hands, then lets gravity take them downward until they slap against the railing. That he's come to court without any evidence seems to be a point of pride. As his exasperation increases, the gestures Tony uses to illustrate it, this repeated raising and lowering of his arms, the twisting of his torso to look over his shoulder and give Justice Smith a look of *Can you believe he just asked that*, have caused him to become dishevelled. The second and third buttons of his shirt have come undone. There is a roll of untucked shirt at his equator. But none of these things makes Tony look as defeated as the sorrowful expression, one that asks for both pity and complicity, which he repeatedly directs toward Sam, the plaintiff.

Sam is dressed much like Tony, only his suit is tailored, cut from more expensive cloth, and doesn't look slept in. He wears a tie and his full Windsor knot is perfect. Sam's hair is parted on the left and sits obediently on his head like a purebred with papers. He looks both fantastic and sleazy, the sort of man whose wife continues to love him specifically because of how much she hates everything about him. Sam does not glance up at the proceedings. He acknowledges neither Tony nor Conrad. He does nothing but move an expensive-looking pen across a pad of crisp white paper housed inside a leather portfolio.

The facts of the case are simple. Sam, the guy making the notes, is a stockbroker working at Eternally Expanding Investments. Tony is, or at least was, a cardiac surgeon—I'm not sure, since he has referred to his profession in both the present and past tense—whose net worth once exceeded $1.7 million. Sam served as Tony's stockbroker for seven and a half years. He's now suing Tony for $25,000 in unpaid commissions. This amount is the absolute ceiling allowed to be sought in small claims court. If Sam wanted just one cent more, they'd all be downtown in civil court, playing with the big boys, not out here in a windowless courtroom wedged into the third floor of a building near the suburbs, literally where the subway ends, on the docket between a woman suing for $2,700 in babysitting fees and a homeowner demanding damages from High and Mighty Interior Design because they painted every wall in his condo the wrong shade of green.

"He recommended to sell Cisco! Google! I had six hundred shares of Google! Do you understand? Do you? Insane! Insane! Insane advice!" Tony's open palm slaps the wooden railing.

"But those were your own tr*aaaaaa*des."

"He gave me his opinion. How can he ask for money for such opinions?"

"But you. Made. Those...tr*aaaaaaaaaaaa*des."

Although he remains on the witness stand, Tony has stopped listening. He's gone somewhere else, mentally checked out, forgotten that he's in a courtroom in the middle of a cross-examination. He stares straight ahead, frozen. The pause is short, maybe three seconds, but long enough for everyone—Conrad, the judge, even Sam, who looks up from his scribbles for the first and only time—to realize that being sued for $25,000 is not the heaviest concern weighing on Tony's mind. This trial may not even make his top five. What these other things are remain undisclosed, but his haunted look, like something very large is moving very quickly toward him, the startled stare of a man accessing something sharp and jagged inside his psyche, scares the fuck out of me.

This morning I called the Howlstein Corporation, asked for an extension on writing the manual for the Gleam 4-19

Automatic Dishwasher, and then invoked the thirteen days of vacation I have banked. I lied to my wife and children as well. As far as my family is concerned, I've rented a temporary office space because I'm overwhelmed by deadlines and am unable to concentrate at my desk in the den, that I need the focus and privacy only an office can provide. My family knows that my occupation is stressful, filled with tight turnarounds and unrealistic expectations, the sort of job where success goes unnoticed and only failure brings attention. That's where they think I am, hard at work, toiling for the good of our nuclear family.

The consequences of this deception will be upon me soon enough. Sometime in the next two or three months, when we gather around the kitchen table and try to decide on a destination for this year's vacation, I will have to admit what I've done. That I've already taken my vacation, that there will be no all-inclusive ten-day stay in Acapulco, or trip to Disneyland, or European tour now that the kids are finally old enough to appreciate it. My wife and children will be angry. They'll call me selfish. I'll take the hit. I am only too aware that if I don't do this, and do it now, there will be no family vacation of any kind this year or any other. If I don't sit here and figure out where all my anger and frustration and aggressively simmering rage are coming from, why I constantly feel unsafe, as if some great disaster perpetually lurks just offstage, waiting for its cue to enter and begin the rampage, if I do not discover what is making me feel this way, I will experience a meltdown that will cause our nuclear family to decay, sending radioactive particles scattering outward, contaminating everything for generations.

There was a time when I wouldn't have hidden what I'm doing from Julie. When she would have been the very first person I'd told. When I would have tried to convince her to come with me. But it's been a while.

I tend to fashion my life into epochs based on the cars we've owned. It seems to me that our love was strongest during the Echo Years, when we lived in a one-bedroom apartment and didn't worry so much. In those days, it would have been unimaginable to discover myself running down the middle of Shaw Street, or any other street, screaming as I chased a kid on a bicycle. I have fond memories of those days, and not just of the sex, or the bohemian-inspired drinking of cheap red wine by candlelight that would continue far into the night because whatever we had to do the next day was of such little importance it could easily be procrastinated without consequence. It's very tempting to romanticize my pre-marriage-and-kids lifestyle, to forget how frustrating those days were, how underused I felt, how the talent I knew I had remained untapped because I didn't have the skills to harness it. But one thing I definitely miss about those one-bedroom-apartment days is the trust I had in my wife's opinion.

It used to be so easy to take in Julie's perspectives and insights, to let those things change the way I saw the world. In the one-bedroom-apartment days, I routinely, without pause or politics, valued her opinion over my own. I turned to her to explain the things I didn't understand.

Take the Lipstick Couple. They weren't exactly street people, but there was something a little off about them. They were the kind of people you could imagine subsisting on social assistance, living in a tiny apartment filled with items it made no sense to keep in the modern day and age, things like typewriters and mannequins and a hatred of capitalism. They were always together. If you saw one, you knew the other was close by. The Lipstick Couple bought a disproportionately large number of apples and cherries at the same corner store where my wife and I bought ramen noodles and popcorn. They ate breakfast late in the afternoon at the diner near our apartment, then spent hours trying to touch the bottoms of bottomless cups of coffee, just like we did. Rarely a day went by without a sighting of the Lipstick Couple.

When we first started noticing them, she never wore any makeup. It was September when she started wearing lipstick, applying a thick coating over her lips, creating a glossy, uninterrupted circle of red. Sometimes she coloured a little bit outside the lines, the lipstick slipping toward her chin or cheeks. Usually there were flecks on her teeth. The look was unsettling, but it didn't become disturbing until I noticed that he'd started wearing lipstick, too. The lipstick he wore was the same shade, but the application wasn't nearly as thick, and his skill at applying it was extremely poor—it was always smeared around his mouth, smudged above and below his lips. His lipstick was so sloppy and haphazard I interpreted it as a sign of mental illness. I grew concerned about him, fearing a period of mental decline that would bring both of them down. I got so worried that I brought it up to Julie.

"There he is," I said. The Lipstick Couple were walking west on Queen, wearing complementary colours. Bright red lipstick was smeared on both of their faces.

"There she is, too." Julie went back to her over-easy eggs.

"I'm worried about him."

"Why?"

"You're not worried about the lipstick?"

"So she likes bright things. She's eccentric. Let her be."

"Not her: him."

"Well, that's the price of love."

"She could at least help him apply it better."

"Wait. What?" That Julie had been only half paying attention to me became clear as she set down her fork.

"Couldn't she at least help him put it on? How hard is that?"

"He's not wearing it. It's from kissing her. He just has it on his mouth because he kisses her so often."

"My marriage is...in jeopardy," Tony says. "Because of his recommendations!"

"No further questions," Conrad says.

"Don't you understand?"

"No further quessssstions!"

Tony comes off the stand, sits at the left end of the wooden table. He does not look over his shoulder to see if his wife is in the courtroom. He has no lawyer. The chair beside him remains empty. His hair needs cutting. His shoes are leather and grey, but one shoelace is black and the other is tan. His fingers clutch the edge of his chair, tightly, as if the world is tilting and he's trying to hold on.

Justice Smith asks for summations. Conrad stands, begins speaking. He holds a single piece of paper that contains bullet points upon which he expands. He speaks well, sums up his case with elegance and brevity, the timbre of his voice alone earning his hourly.

"Your summation?" Justice Smith prompts Tony.

Tony looks up. He stands, takes from a red nylon backpack some papers that he holds in his hand but doesn't look at.

"He lost all of my money. I can't pay him for that. Can I?"

"Anything else you want to tell me? Anything more... judicial?"

"That's what I got," Tony replies.

Justice Smith nods, closes the file in front of him, explains that his decision will be reserved, that he will set a date to read his verdict in open court.

"Pe*rrrrr*haps. If we could set a date now? Would that be possible?"

Justice Smith nods, flips through a datebook, looks up. "I'm here on October 30. How about October 30? Ten o'clock? I'll make it top of the docket."

Conrad produces his own datebook, leather-bound. He flips pages backward and forward as Sam takes out a Blackberry, presses buttons. Leaning close, they consult in quiet tones. Then they both nod, and Conrad stands.

"October 30 would be fine," Conrad says. "Ten a.m."

Justice Smith looks at the defendant. Tony stands. I can't see his face, only the back of his head. He has produced neither a phone nor datebook. He looks at the floor. The silence is the only thing that makes him look back up. Tony sees that Justice Smith is staring at him. He turns to the left and sees that Jason and Conrad have made him the centre of their attention as well. Tony takes a blue disposable pen from the inside pocket of his blazer, opens his left hand, and spreads out his fingers. He scribbles on his hand, presumably the date of his next court appearance, in handwriting that slopes downward, a lifeline in quick descent, composed of information that will soon be washed away.

PART TWO

ONLY THE CAPTAIN MAY
LOWER THE LIFEBOATS

The wedding chapel on the fourth floor of Toronto City Hall is an oasis of flowing white curtains and dark wooden furniture surrounded by twenty-three storeys of concrete, glass, and steel. In this regard, the wedding chapel is like marriage itself: a small, organic core encased in functionality. The chapel, although in a public space, is privately run. Weddings are not open to the public, although anyone can attend: they just have to be invited by the bride and groom. When I find myself sharing the elevator with a wedding party, I take it as a sign, tell the bride and groom that I'm writing an article on city hall weddings for the *Globe and Mail*. To my surprise, they agree to allow my presence. Is it my cynicism that made me think an act of such inclusiveness would be unlikely? Or is their openness sparked by nothing more than vanity at the prospect of having their wedding covered by the *Globe and Mail*? The significance of this question increases exponentially as the elevator continues to rise.

There are ten people in this wedding party, and their nervous energy, combined with the sly smiles they pass amongst themselves, make it clear that they're unable to think of marriage as anything other than the ultimate expression of love and romance. As the elevator rises above the third floor, an unexpected and reverential silence overtakes them. The only sound is the motor pulling the cables. Then, the bell dings. The doors open. The bride, groom, and their various attendants spill out of the elevator, a tipped carton of black suits and new dresses and hopes for a brighter tomorrow.

Their laughter bounces off the high ceiling and concrete walls as they pull open the heavy glass doors of the wedding chapel and sit on the leather benches lining both sides of the foyer, organizing themselves by gender, girls on one side and boys on the other. At the top of the benches, closest to the doors of the chapel, which remain closed, the bride and groom face each other. The groom, Sergei, has a sharp, strong jaw and freshly cut short-cropped black hair. His suit is pressed. His tied is knotted in a full Windsor. Sergei adjusts the single white rose pinned to his lapel, then looks across the aisle, catches his bride's eye, and smiles.

The bride, Calina, returns Sergei's smile with an intensity that's impossible to sustain, causing her to look down at the points of her shiny white shoes. She adjusts her firm grip on the bouquet of white roses that she holds, and will continue to hold, over her belly. Calina's body is athletic, her tan won through hours on the tennis court or jogging or playing *pétanque* or whatever sport it is that her youth and confidence allows her to excel at. She watches Sergei bend down and wipe an invisible spot from the toe of his left shoe, then reach into his inside pocket and pull out a pack of chewing gum.

"Камедь?" he asks in Russian.

"*Obrigado*," she replies in Portuguese.

This is the thing. Between them, this couple can communicate in six languages. The problem is that English is the only one they share, and neither is very good with it. So the question I have—and forgive me, but there is no unsentimental way to put it—can two people without a common tongue really fall in love?

It's a cynical question, but I'm feeling cynical today, primarily because my teeth have begun rotting in my head. I'm not being metaphorical. Last night I was sitting on the couch, feeling lazy and dysfunctional because I'd spent the one hour I had to myself watching a *Law & Order* repeat instead of throwing my efforts behind another attempt to fix *Forgive Us Our Eccentricities as We Forgive the Eccentricities of Others*. As I watched the show, already knowing who the murderer was, I replayed in my head the fight I'd just had with Julie, trying to figure out who was to blame for transforming the task of determining what to watch on television into an allegory for our sixteen-year-old relationship. And then I felt something tiny and hard in my mouth. I spit a shiny piece of white onto my palm. Several moments passed before I realized it was a piece of tooth.

My curious tongue ran itself along the bottom of my teeth until it found the absence, the rough patch missing on the left side of my right wisdom tooth. There wasn't any pain, but my tongue couldn't stop running itself over the ragged edge, as if some primal part of my unconscious believed that enough rubbing could counteract the damage and eliminate the need for a dentist. I wrapped the bit of tooth in a Kleenex, like you would a bug you're saving to show the exterminator, as evidehhhhhhnce, and put it in the top drawer of my desk.

The next morning, this morning, there wasn't enough pain to prevent me from pretending everything was fine. I walked my kids to school, then I went up to the subway, prepared to go to small claims court. Nothing seemed out of the ordinary until, standing on the Bloor/Yonge platform, I lost my belief that everything was going to be all right. My heart began to speed. My lungs couldn't pull in enough air. Everyone stood too close to me, and I couldn't look any of them in the eyes. Significant concentration was required to stop myself from screaming, from issuing a pre-semantic growl that would, without words, tell everyone to step the fuck back, to leave me alone, to allow me a few precious seconds to pull myself together. But what scared me even more than the justifiable belief that I was losing my grip on sanity was, that no one noticed. Not even those standing so close to me that I could name the fabric of their clothes became aware of how tightly my hands had turned to fists, how pale my skin was or the beads of sweat dotting my forehead. Dr. Jekyll was turning into Mr. Hyde beside them, as they waited for the north-bound train to arrive, and it was just another day.

This is when the idea of going to the wedding chapel at city hall, instead of small claims court, leapt into my mind. I don't know where it came from. I'm willing to believe it was truly inspired, a correcting nudge from God, the divine fist hitting a 1970s television set in order to improve reception. Wherever the idea came from, it was a life preserver splashing into the Sea of Insecurity that was pulling me under. I pushed through the shoulder-to-shoulder rush-hour crowd, ran up the stairs, over to the south platform, and caught the next train down to the Queen stop.

The wedding chapel doors burst open and, without grooms-men, bridesmaids, or family, a freshly minted marriage emerges. Radiating joy and confidence, they cut between Calina and Sergei, making their way out into the hallway, where the only thing holding them back from starting their new life together is the arrival of the elevator. Calina and Sergei stare at this marriage, three minutes old. It is unclear whether their immovable gaze is prompted by envy or gratitude, but they remain so transfixed that when the officiant arrives, she has to gently touch Sergei's shoulder to gain his attention.

The officiant is an owl-like woman who carries her plumpness with a buoyant grace. She begins to explain the stages of the ceremony, her hands drifting through the air like kites on the winds of matrimony. Calina looks at Sergei. Sergei holds up his hand, open palm.

"Please be slow. English is second to us both," Sergei says.

"Of course. My apologies." The officiant is receptive. She marries, on average, twelve couples a day, and the idea of a couple lacking a language in common registers low on the list of impediments. But more than that, the officiant long ago learned not to question anyone's motives, not to judge, to embrace the statistics; since four out of ten marriages end in divorce, even for Calina and Sergei, the odds are on their side. Using simple sentences, the officiant walks through the stages of the ceremony—the vows, the rings, the document that must be signed. In less than five minutes, only one question remains.

"Would you like to make a grand entrance? Or would you two like to come in together?" the officiant asks. Calina does not understand. She looks at Sergei.

"Me here, then you to enter?" Sergei opens his hand, points to the tips of his fingers and then to the base of his palm. "Or the same?" He uses his pointer and middle finger to walk across his palm.

"The same!" Calina's face lights up. She takes Sergei's arm.

The officiant ushers the bridesmaids and groomsmen into the chamber, shows them where to stand. She aims a remote control at a spot in the ceiling and pre-recorded classical music begins to play. I hang back, trying to make myself inconspicuous. My efforts are wasted: they've already forgotten about me completely. When the bridesmaids and groomsmen finish arranging themselves at the front of the chapel, the officiant once again aims the remote at the ceiling and a fluttering graceful Mozart begins to play. Two or three seconds later, the bride and groom come in, arm in arm, together.

This is where my anxiety returns. It is as pervasive and crushing as it was on the subway platform. I want to run away, but the chapel doors are closed. A hasty exit would require opening them, a gesture so obvious and interruptive it would be impossible not to interpret it as a statement. Even so, I still consider doing it: the only reason I don't is that I don't have the nerve. As the handsome groom and the beautiful bride look lovingly at each other, their perfectly blue eyes sparkling from the middle of their symmetrical faces, I struggle very hard to remain silent, to stop myself from taking a deep breath and yelling, "It will not always be this way!

"Yes, you have love! No doubt! And it feels as forever as sunsets and rainbows, but it won't always be! Either something horrible will happen to one of you, or both of you, or to your kids, or you won't even be able to have kids, or one of you will and the other won't, but some tragedy will befall you! And as your feet are kicked out from under you, sending you tumbling into a spiral of despair, blame, and disappointment, the love you feel right now will be taken down, too.

"Or nothing will happen, which is even worse, because then you will have to sit there, watching, powerless, from the other side of an empty room that you are, for invisible reasons, unable to cross as your love evaporates. Your love will leave you one molecule at a time, like water left in a boiling pot, the love that was once stronger than anything you'd ever felt in your entire life turning into steam, floating away until all of it's gone. The pot will boil dry and all you'll have left is the pungent calcium stink of overheated metal."

What gives me the strength not to say any of these things is observing how tightly Sergei keeps his arm around Calina. I stare at his arm. I know that if he moves it, if he lets go, I will begin screaming. And I get lucky—the only time he lets go is to take her hands as they exchange vows.

"I do," Sergei says in his thick Russian accent.

"I do," Calina says in her thick Portuguese accent.

They kiss, deeply. Hand in hand, they move to a small table, where Sergei keeps his right hand on the small of Calina's back as she signs the marriage licence. She keeps her left hand on Sergei's shoulder as he signs. Their arms encircle each other's waists as they pose for pictures.

What happened to true love? There was a time when questioning the reality of that concept was unthinkable. The existence of true love was undeniable, and those who couldn't believe in it were to be pitied, handled gently, like baby birds fallen from nests. Capitalism and science have combined to liquidate romance from our concept of love. Romance was sold off to the highest bidder so that desire could be marketed as genetics, lovers perceived as partners, the bed transformed into a boardroom table. Marriage has become nothing but a mutually beneficial merger, featuring terms negotiated through combined earning potential and the division of labour.

My perspective on love has been so corrupted that I can't even remember what I thought true love was supposed to be. A soulmate? The idea that the perfect person is out there, waiting to be found? That God made a whole, then split it in two, scattering the parts as some sort of metaphysical scavenger hunt? These ideas are ludicrous, but metaphorically correct. I don't believe in true love because I no longer believe that a person should need someone else to be whole. I've been conditioned to believe that I must function on my own, that if I'm not absolutely independent, I'm broken. The notion of love itself is increasingly difficult to believe in. What economic sense does love make? It doesn't contribute to a stable emotional environment. Love does the opposite. It makes me vulnerable and frail and submissive to another's will. I miss being those things, even if culture tells me they're worthless. The idea that love can be free of self-interest and functionality is such a beautiful, optimistic thought, having so little to do with the real estate market or gross domestic product, that I'm not surprised it's fallen out of fashion.

Love hasn't changed. We have.

Sergei and Calina are certainly looking at each other like they believe in true love. As they leave the chapel, they don't look back at the officiant. They don't even look at the groomsmen and the bridesmaids. They look only at each other. They have not stopped touching since they were still girlfriend and boyfriend. They race down the foyer, cutting between the next bride and groom, and then they're through the glass doors. The elevator arrives and they step inside. The rest of the wedding party waits for the next one. As the doors close, Sergei and Calina are still holding hands, happy, elated, firm in their understanding that these thirty minutes have changed their lives forever. They are an inspiration to believe in love, to reclaim a belief in true love, and yet my tongue, my restless independent tongue, continues to run over the broken side of my tooth, again and again, as if to say, *We'll see, we'll fucking well see. Decay is inevitable. Nothing can withstand it: nothing at all.*

06. SUPPOSED CURES & BATTLE PLANS

The clock in room 337 emits the same electric hum as all of the others, but the minute hand doesn't sweep—it jumps, filling the courtroom with a predicable yet still surprising CLICK every sixty seconds. Both defendants, Frank and Brad, have noticed. Frank, sitting in the middle of the long wooden table on the left, marks each second with a tap of his weathered brown shoe, then executes a heel stomp when the hand CLICKS forward. Beside him, Brad, with a thin smile on his lips and an even thinner moustache underneath, nods as Frank stomps. The CLICK also triggers the tip of my tongue to run along the jagged edge of the broken tooth. All three of us commit these gestures nine more times, silently, without acknowledging that we're doing them until Lance, the plaintiff, arrives.

Lance is a very tall man with a beer gut just coming into bloom, who wears a blue suit, black tie, and fashionable shoes. He sets a bulging manila envelope on top of the wooden table on the right. The court reporter disappears into the back room. Moments later, she ushers in Justice Remington and we all stand.

Justice Remington is thin and old. His side-parted white hair has been brushed so perfectly that there's a sense of tension to it, as if at any moment it could suddenly snap upward like a bear trap. He takes small steps. He pretty much falls into his chair. He twirls sideways and lets momentum carry him until he's facing all of us. He does all these things and yet, somehow, maintains his judicial authority. Just seeing him like that, his eyes magnified and blinking behind the thick lenses of his black-framed glasses, makes me fall a little bit in love with him.

Justice Remington studies the plaintiff and the defendants. His shoulders slump, as if he is experiencing a slow leak. The cause of this isn't clear. It could be because both parties are self-represented. Possibly it's the way everybody continually refuses to look at each other. Or maybe it's some sort of judicial sixth sense, the hard-won ability to smell pettiness in the air. Whatever the motivation, the sigh Justice Remington releases causes him to become just a little more deflated. He looks over his shoulder at the clock. It CLICKS. Although his eyes and shoulders don't move, his hands rise and fall. They do the shrugging for him.

"Let's try to stay calm. Everyone will have a full opportunity to give their side of things. It will be hard, but let's not become argumentative."

Lance takes the stand and gets sworn in. His story is not a complicated one, although he does seem to go on and on. A professional bus driver and tour guide, Lance took his Honda Odyssey into the dealership that Frank manages. The minivan needed an oil change and had a slow leak in the front right tire. Forty minutes later the work was done, Lance paid $168.07, and everyone was happy. But as Lance drove off the lot, he noticed a flashing light on the dashboard. Returning to the service station, Lance called it to the attention of a mechanic, Brad, who told him this was standard. Brad explained that there was a sensor inside the tire and that the light would go off after he drove for a while.

It didn't.

Three weeks later, Lance returned to the dealership, complaining that the light was still on. Brad told Lance the same thing—that it was a sensor in the tire, that it would eventually go off. So Frank did more driving. The light continued to stay on. This bugged the bejesus out of Lance, so he took his minivan to another mechanic, where the sensor was replaced for $56.

"When was this?" Justice Remington asks, proving me wrong in assuming that he wasn't really paying attention—that he, like everyone else in this courtroom had drifted off.

"July 3, 2012," Lance answers.

"You waited six months?"

"Yes."

"And the light was on the whole time?"

There is more than a little accusation in the voice Justice Remington uses to ask this question. Enough to make Lance pause and rethink the answer that was already on the tip of his tongue. And that's the thing about small claims court. Things are more casual here; it's the judicial equivalent of spending time with a father who has access every other weekend. Whereas in civil court or family court, the justices strive to create the appearance of neutrality, here in small claims they allow more of their true feelings to bubble to the surface. They say what they're thinking. I don't know if this is official policy, but I have no other explanation for the disdain, the almost teenage sarcasm, that empowers the deeper registers of Justice Remington's voice.

"It was six months later and the repair cost you $56?" Justice Remington says, and I fall in love with him a little bit more.

"That's right."

"Then why is your claim is for $3,000?"

"With the company I run, I charge $150 an hour. So I added it all up. That's how I got $3,000."

"You're tallying twenty hours?"

"Yes."

"You're asking them for twenty hours of your time?"

"That includes the money I spent..."

"That's $56?"

"And what I paid before."

"That's...$200? So...$2,800 is for your lost time?"

"Correct."

"How do you figure you spent nineteen hours of time?"

"I have a four-hour minimum."

On this, Lance rests his case. Justice Remington's hands make the shrugging motion. He looks over his shoulder at the clock. It CLICKS. Frank, who's wearing a three-piece suit like it's a Halloween costume, begins his cross. His voice struggles to hide frustration as he asks a list of prepared questions. The information they elicit is exactly the same as what Lance has volunteered, facts that are revealed for a third and final time when Frank mounts his defence. At the end of which, Lance has no questions, and both parties rest.

"Let's have a forty-five-minute recess," Justice Remington says. He stands, turns his back to us, and exits.

It was my neighbour, Samantha, who told me about Dr. Nashid. I was outside on the porch, breathing deeply because I no longer smoke, when she returned from walking her dog, a beloved nine-year-old lab named Ramone, whose hips have pretty much fused and who has to be carried upstairs. I like my neighbour a lot. We have children roughly the same age. Sam lets them play video games and occasionally loses her cool and yells at them. I do these things, too, and it was a great relief to learn I wasn't the only one. I see child-raising as a craft, whereas most of the parents in this part of Toronto consider it an art; I want my kids to go out and serve a useful role in society, instead of spending their lives in a white-walled cube, surrounded by security because they're precious.

I'm not sure why I told Sam about my tooth. I had never told her anything that personal before. I think I hoped she'd say my strategy of leaving the chipped tooth alone, that doing of nothing, was appropriate. That is not what happened. I told her the story of watching TV and spitting out the white something and discovering it was a piece of wisdom tooth.

"Did they pull it?"

"Who?"

"Your dentist!"

"I haven't gone yet."

"What?"

"Um..."

"You have to go to the dentist. Like...today. Seriously. What are you thinking?"

I wanted to tell Sam that I realized how ludicrous, stupid, and unreasonable I'm being. That I am fully aware of how anyone who avoids potentially painful situations will surely soon enter the only state nature can't abide: stagnation. But one of the few powers that's grown stronger during this journey into middle age is my uncanny ability to endure pain in small increments. I would rather withstand tiny repeated moments of pain than face one massive dose of it, even if it could potentially end the suffering. This goes for my teeth, my job, and my marriage. Conventional wisdom attributes this attitude to growing weak and fearful. I do not agree. Not at all. The difficulty I'm having taking potentially beneficial risks isn't because the courage of my youth has faded, but because I'm smarter. I know that all those supposed cures and battle plans fail way more often than they succeed. God loves irony: more often than not it is the attempted cure, the final invasion, that brings about absolute demise.

If my many years have taught me anything, it's that victory is not assured. Twenty years ago, victory wasn't even a variable. It was a given. Ten years ago, sure, I had some doubts, victory was taking much longer to arrive than I'd anticipated, but I still considered it to pre-exist at some point in the future, and all I had to do was continue moving toward it. This assumption made leaps of faith easy, rendered even the largest amounts of pain—broken hearts and shattered dreams—easy to endure. I could fall in love again, find another dream job to apply for, because my faith in a beneficial outcome was rock-steady. The use of a blindfold as a risk-management strategy may not be wise, but it sure is effective. Only, I can't fool myself anymore. There's a hole in the blindfold and through it I can see that there's no guarantee of success, that even goals based on a solid belief in one's abilities, combined with a realistic understanding of your personal limits, don't guarantee victory. I know that if you build it, there's a very good chance it will sit empty forever, slowly rotting, a monument to naïveté and self-delusion. If you have enough money, you can avoid taxes and delay death, but no one can live a life without failure.

The last time I went to the dentist was eight years ago, in 2004, the year in which my faith in victory first began to exhibit signs of decay. My phobia, if you want to call it that, isn't provoked by needles and shiny metal instruments on shiny steel trays—although I am afraid of these things—but by an inability to believe that dentistry can retard the corrosion of middle age, that even the pain suffered in the name of oral hygiene can elicit a positive result.

Julie has repeatedly informed me that this is my solution to everything, that my default position is the doing of nothing, that I trust inaction over my own abilities, and just let it all slide. What she doesn't understand is that my methods aren't procrastination or avoidance or even laziness, but rather an acceptance that we are powerless against the forces of creation. No matter how much we want something, or how much effort we use to obtain it, victory is out of our hands. The world will have its way with us no matter how much we struggle.

In my twenties and thirties, this strategy functioned as a positive force. I was willing to let—in fact, I relished letting—the world carry me wherever it wanted me to be. But in the last eight years, something changed. The world and I had a falling out. A thousand tiny disappointments, events too small to be described as defeats, forced a distance between us. I lost my faith in the world. I stopped believing that the world was on my side, that it had my best interests at heart. When facing situations in which I need to be vulnerable, in which I could potentially be hurt, situations like a trip to the dentist or telling my wife how much I love and need her, I now assume that there will be pain, and that it'll be both excruciating and useless.

If you have too little faith in the world, you end up fearing everything; if you have too much, you turn into an asshole. My ability to locate a middle ground between these two poles, a land balanced between fear and pride, self-confidence and self-delusion, has been rendered inept by all the bad things I've seen happen to good people, the endless repetition of the best of intentions leading to nothing but failure and heartache. The needle of my internal compass does nothing but spin around and around and around.

And that's why I'm afraid of going to the dentist.

Sam saw the fear on my face. She handed me the end of Ramone's leash and went inside her house. She returned with a white, slightly bent business card that she handed to me. On it, in Helvetica, was the name, address, and phone number of a dentist. The letters were not raised. The card stock wasn't thick.

"Go see her."

"Why this one?"

"Because she's the dentist for people who are afraid to go to the dentist."

I nodded. I didn't say anything. My tongue found the jagged edge of the broken tooth and I took the business card, although I held it between my thumb and index finger, away from my body like a Kleenex containing something communicable. Sam let out a slight grunt as she picked up Ramone and carried him up the steps and onto the porch.

During the recess, as I sit in the overheated hallway making these notes, I see Justice Remington waiting for the elevator. I wait beside him. When it arrives, we both step inside. He doesn't recognize me. We travel to the main floor, ignoring each other. I walk toward the washroom, then at the last minute do an about-face and follow him into the small cafeteria. Sitting on the other side of the room, I watch him order a coffee, add two sugars, then sit down at a table and read the Wheels section of the *Toronto Star*, which someone has left behind.

Justice Remington gives his full attention to the newspaper. At this moment, the only act of serious contemplation concerning him is the purchase of a new Honda. While everyone involved in the trial thinks he's locked himself inside some book-lined room, weighing the evidence, he's here drinking coffee in a cafeteria with orange plastic chairs and a display fridge that offers four different brands of bottled water. Is he wrong to do this? Or is he brilliant? Is he aware that calling a forty-five-minute recess is just as important as his black robes and the elevation of the desk he sits behind? He must be. You can say that it's all theatre, artifice, but those are necessary to construct and maintain authority. Yes, it's all manufactured, but that doesn't mean it isn't real. Has no one else ever noticed that most people use the word *authentic* as a synonym for *harder*? Just what is it that makes being poor more authentic than being rich? Sadness more authentic than joy? How exactly is living on the seventeenth floor of a condo less authentic than living in a slum next to a dump? One is fantastic and the other is horrible, but both have equal claim to the adjective in question.

To me, it all smacks of the self-hating middle class, those who feel guilty about living in never-before-seen comfort, for having good nutrition, health care, and relative safety for their children. We shouldn't be calling this inauthentic: we should be honouring it, praising this tiny slice in our species' history, this handful of years where it's at least unlikely to have to watch your children starve to death, or die before age ten of some otherwise curable disease, or get lynched for being gay or black or capable of giving birth. Where the ideas of murder and rape are slightly less fashionable. The sin is that the whole world doesn't have these privileges, and that we're not fighting harder to make this happen. The idea that a comfortable life isn't an authentic one is nothing but a remnant of Christianity, a dysfunctional devotion sustained through a belief that suffering brings redemption. Which it doesn't. It's just suffering. All suffering brings is more suffering.

Justice Remington finishes his coffee, takes a silver pen out of his inner pocket, and makes notes in a black pocket-sized Moleskine. I use my phone to time him. It takes him two minutes and thirty-six seconds to compose his verdict. Leaving the Wheels section behind, he takes the elevator to the third floor and returns to courtroom 337 forty-seven minutes after he left it. The clock CLICKS. We all stand, and then we sit, and then he takes the black Moleskine from his pocket. Lance looks surprisingly confident. Frank's finger worries against the nail of his thumb. Brad smiles in antici-pation, as if this is a Hollywood blockbuster he's waited all summer to see.

"The plaintiff presents a position that I find completely unaccountable, completely without merit. No rule of law, no proof, no cause of action requiring lost time. It is so far-fetched that I cannot give it any credence and I have no hesitation in dismissing this claim. I am awarding the defen-dants $300 each for costs incurred from self-representation. Is there anything further?"

"No," says Frank.

"No," says Brad.

Lance doesn't reply. Then he nods. Justice Remington does the hand shrug thing again and leaves. The three of them sit alongside each other, waiting for copies of the ver-dict. They don't talk. The clock CLICKS three times before the court reporter returns and hands each of them a piece of paper, which they all use both hands to hold, like school-children.

"Good work," Lance says. "Congratulations."

There doesn't seem to be any irony or sarcasm in Lance's voice. He's sincere. Lance stands there for a couple of CLICKS. If a hand had been extended, he would gladly have shaken it. But no hand is extended. With confident motions that indicate a firm belief the world is still on his side, Lance folds the verdict length-wise, puts it in his manila envelope, and leaves.

Brad slaps his buddy on the back.

"What an asshole," Frank says.

07. LUKE & LEIA

It's been eighty-three days.

Eighty-three days since what? Where are you?

Since we've slept in the same bed.

Where are you?

I'm not exactly sure how to respond to this. Does she really think I'm out of the house? That I've decided to hit the town instead of falling asleep with the TV on, then sneaking shoeless up the stairs, as quietly as possible, pausing in front of our bedroom, taking the closed door as a physical manifestation of all that is still between us and moving on to the guest room? It's so obvious to me that I'm still in the house that her question provokes a flash of anger.

Do you mean physically or emotionally?
Downstairs.

You're counting?

Don't you think it's romantic of me?

I think it's sad.

I do, too.
Why don't we stop it?

The screen displays no new words. The cursor flashes. I count to thirty. I check my email. I have no new messages. When I return to our conversation, the three lines are blinking, indicating that she's typing.

She types for a very long time

It's not up to me.

I wonder what her original response was, the one she decided not to send, that she censored. Since it was made of ones and zeroes, it technically never existed in the first place, and is now lost forever. Or maybe that's a perspective provided by my age, a residue of ink on paper, the idea that something only truly exists if it can be touched, experienced, which would also explain why the idea of us sleeping next to each other is so important to me.

It's up to me?

I really don't want to get into this. I'm tired.

Okay.

There's a green dot beside her name so I know she's still online. I check my email again. I google my name. I look up the lyrics of a Pixies song that's been in my head for days and days. When I go back to our conversation, the green dot is still there.

Want to hear something crazy?
Hey?
Did I tell you about my teeth?

Your teeth?

> *A big hunk came out of the side of my wisdom tooth.*
> *I'm going to the dentist for the first*
> *time in years tomorrow morning.*

How much is this costing?

> *Really?*
> *Honestly?*
> *That's what you want to know?*

It's expensive. That's all.

> *That doesn't impress you?*
> *That I faced my fear?*

If you'd done it in the nineties.

I throw the phone, but not hard. It lands at the end of the bed. I turn out the lamp, pull up the covers, and stare at the ceiling. A rectangular-based cone of cellphone light illuminates the room. It is unnatural, the colour blue trapped inside ice. I feel unsafe, like my marriage is a loose tooth hanging by a thread that my tongue can't stop playing with. The light disappears, but I'm still awake. I know that it's a mistake to have let visiting the dentist slide for so long. I know it's indicative of all the mistakes I've made. That when I was offered a full-time job at CBC, I didn't take it. That when my first book had the moderate success it did, I didn't write a sequel, hubris promoting me to write something deeper and harder and vastly less popular instead. When our children were born, I didn't scrounge for a stable job but continued working freelance, providing an insufficient and unstable income for our growing family, a significant financial slack that Julie was forced to pick up. And, vastly more significant, when she did go out and find work and make something of herself, I did not tell her how wonderful she was to do this, how proud and frankly in awe of her it made me. I sit up in bed, reach for my phone, and turn it back on. There's a message waiting.

I wish you'd faced all your fears years ago.

This is what makes me believe we should continue trying to work this out. Beyond any psychological damage a divorce would do to Jack and Jenny, surpassing the expense of lawyers or the depression brought on by basement apartments filled with new disposable furniture, what really makes me believe that Julie and I should fight to stay together is the fact that we are still fighting, that we still so effectively get under each other's skin.

What I don't know is whether holding this up, giving it the significance of some kind of holy relic of matrimony, is derived from strength or weakness. Am I revering the power of love or denying the knowledge that ours has devolved into a brother-and-sister relationship, Luke and Leia, something as devoid of passion as it is filled with bickering and rivalries? While I'm still trying to put all of these things into a text, one from her arrives.

I need you to be stronger. More confident. I can't take care of you all the time. That's what I'm doing. You think I'm retreating but I'm not. I'm learning how to take care of myself. That's all. That's it. To be there for myself.

                                              Because I can't be there for you?

Yes.

                                             That's pretty harsh.

Is it?

  I'm there for you. All the time. I feel like I live my life for you.

You're there when you want to be there for me. When it's easy. When it's something that you want to do. You're there in the ways that you want to be there. But you're not there for me, like I need you to be, not really.

                                            One hundred days.

Hey?

                           If we haven't figured this out in one hundred days,
                                        we should call it quits.

You know what you've just done, right?
Do you?

                              What? Tell me what horrible thing I've done.

You've made sure it won't ever happen.
Good night.
Don't come up.

                                        Wasn't planning on it.

The defendant, Monica, has covered the long wooden table on the left with pages of lined three-ring loose-leaf paper. She moves them around, stacks them in piles, staples them together in clumps. She makes notes on them with a disposable pen. Her handwriting is flowery, full of loops and flourishes, a style that could very well include a tendency to dot her i's with hearts. Monica is so preoccupied with her note-making that she doesn't notice Justice Royal's arrival. The rest of us are already standing when she raises her head. She begins to rise as we sit down. For a second, maybe even two, Monica stands all on her own.

Diane, the plaintiff, wears no earrings, necklaces, or jewellery of any kind. The only object on the surface of the long wooden table she sits behind is a tabbed document, six inches thick. Her posture is worthy of a caryatid and she stares straight ahead. She doesn't look bored exactly; rather, her expression indicates she's concentrating on a menial task, perhaps composing a list of phone calls that need to be returned.

"How many witnesses?" Justice Royal asks Monica.

"Just me."

"And you, Ms. Davison?"

"One. Mr. Ted Winters."

"Very well."

Ted Winters walks from among the spectators to the witness stand. He's tall, but keeps his shoulders hunched as he gets sworn in, as if he's trying to make himself smaller.

Diane smiles. She opens the bound document and flips to the green tab about an inch and a half from the cover. In a brisk, efficient voice, Diane begins a line of questioning, which quickly establishes that Ted works for Mutual Benefits and his specialty is securing retroactive income tax credits.

"Was Monica Rhonda your client?"

"She was."

"Did you meet with her in June of last year?"

"Yes."

"What was this meeting about?"

"A disability tax credit."

"About Ms. Rhonda getting one?"

"Yes."

"How did you help her?"

"We assisted her doctor…"

"Dr. David Wellington?"

"Right. That's right."

"Please continue."

"We assisted Dr. David Wellington with filling out a beneficiary claim, which we then submitted."

"What was the purpose of this form?"

"To prove that Ms. Rhonda was eligible for a disability credit refund."

"On her taxes?"

"Correct."

"What happened on May 13 of this year?"

"We were no longer authorized to view Monica's account."

"Who originally gave you permission to view her account?"

"She did."

"She?"

"Ms. Rhonda."

"Who revoked this permission?"

"Monica…Ms. Rhonda."

"What happened on May 15?"

"Revenue Canada granted her a disability credit and

issued a refund of $4,378.11."

"Do you feel this refund was the result of your work?"

"Definitely. We filled out the form. We sent it in."

"Did you receive any remuneration for this work?"

"We did not."

"Thank you."

Using the tip of an unpainted fingernail, Diane closes her tabbed document. Her only witness widens his stance and pulls back his shoulders as he prepares to be cross-examined. The only thing that stops Monica from asking her first question is the sound of Justice Royal clearing his throat.

"What is your percentage?" Justice Royal's voice and eyebrows rise as he asks this question.

Ted looks at Diane. She nods. Ted hunches his shoulders before he answers. "Twenty-five percent."

"I see."

Let me point out right here that this case, which requires a justice, a bailiff, a court reporter, a courtroom, furniture, lights, heat and electricity, a building, someone to vacuum the carpets and empty the wastepaper basket, professionals educated through a heavily subsidized secondary educational system, not to mention the roads, subways, and buses we all used to get to this out-of-the-way location, is being fought over $1,149.23, including GST.

"No further questions."

Diane sits as Monica stands, their heads moving like kids on a see-saw. Monica picks up several different pieces of paper, all of which she sets back down. She attempts a smile, but the effort is forced and only succeeds at revealing her crooked yellow teeth.

"What I'm— Asking— Isn't it— What— I'm really nervous," Monica says.

"The majority of us are nervous."

It seems like a strange thing for Justice Royal to say, but it's also what Monica needs to hear. She closes her eyes. Her face expresses determination as she pulls in a deep breath. Moving her left hand behind her back, she crosses her fingers. Whether this is for luck or to enable her to lie remains unseen.

Three other people are waiting with me, but I have been here the longest. It surprises me that I've lasted this long without grabbing my coat and running east down Queen Street, laughing manically at my newfound freedom. It seems unlikely that I will manage to contain my fear and continue sitting in this vinyl-covered, armless chair until the pretty dental assistant with the curly black hair calls my name, then leads me down some unnaturally sterile hallway to a room I'm sure will be windowless, where a tilting leather chair sits in the exact centre, beside a tray where sharp silver instruments have been set out in rows like dead soldiers made of shiny metal.

I am a coward, but here's what I've learned about heroes: every single one of them is a con man. I admit that heroes are better than I am, that they're stronger, tougher, more worthy of respect and admiration and love than I ever will be. But they are not without fear. When encountering danger, the self-preservation instinct inside them yells that they should run away and flee to safety just as loudly as it does in me. Heroes are simply capable of pushing this voice down, smothering it beneath layers of self-discipline and denial, until it's silenced completely. This is what gives them the ability to continue on toward danger instead of away from it.

Chuck Yeager, the first man to break the sound barrier in an experimental plane called the X-1, was plagued by nightmares. There are a couple of things you need to know about the X-1 to fully understand the significance of Chuck Yeager's dreams. The first is that it was designed in the shape of a bullet, which didn't allow for an escape hatch—it would have ruined the aerodynamics. The second is that the X-1 burned so much fuel that the vast majority of the plane's body doubled as a gas tank. Some people describe the X-1 as a bullet with wings: in reality, it was a gas tank with wings. Yet every day Yeager flew it, pushing the plane beyond its limits, trying to make it go faster and faster. And each time Yeager went up into the sky, he knew he was sitting on top of a bomb, and that should anything go wrong, he had no escape route.

Every night Yeager went home and slept beside his beautiful wife and was woken up by horrible nightmares, wherein the X-1 burst into flame and he was burned alive inside it. It's not that Yeager felt safe inside that cockpit—he just didn't get around to feeling his fear until much later. I've done that in reverse. Whereas Yeager used his ability to ignore, or at least temporary redirect, his fear in order to achieve greatness, I've used that very same technique to achieve mediocrity. I've used it to sustain my denial of decay—in my teeth, my marriage, and my life. I've used the strategies of a hero to become a coward.

When the pretty black-haired dental assistant calls my name, I look at the guy beside me. Several seconds pass before I admit who I am and follow her down a hallway, walking beneath six florescent tubes, three sets of two, and into a room that turns out to be windowless. The dentist's chair is white and looks like leather, but isn't. On the far wall is a Monet print, a lily-pad jumble of pinks and greens that, although it's one of my favourite paintings by one of my favourite painters, provokes seasickness. I sit in the chair. A blue napkin of thick paper is tied around my neck. Beads of sweat pop through my skin like air bubbles in boiling water. My hands become fists. I close my eyes, but it feels like the world is suddenly sloping to the right and I open them just in time to see a pointed metal spear inches from my eyeballs.

"Can you open a little wider?" Dr. Nashid has an Egyptian accent, the body of a long-distance runner, and the ability to see the fear in my eyes. Her voice becomes gentle, compassionate, and I open my mouth wider.

"I'll have to have it a bit more open still."

"I'm not sure my mouth can open that much more."

Dr. Nashid sets down the tiny silver spear. Her gloved right hand rests on my chin, pushes gently downward. Then she turns the lamp so that the glare is all I can see. As I close my eyes, it becomes vitally important she understands that as a teenager, I believed in God. That this faith then dwindled until I was in my twenties and all I believed in were people. That my faith has kept losing power, and now that I'm closer to fifty than forty, the only belief I can sustain is in the absolute self-centredness of humanity; that our basic selfishness has prompted us to build a society with just enough justice to keep most of us safe. I need her to know, desperately, that I'm afraid of losing this last shred of my faith, that should I stop believing this, if my fingertips lose their tenuous grip on the ledge of plausible deniability as the rest of my consciousness dangles over the endless gulf of pessimism, I really don't know what I'm going to do. That the decay of my teeth seems like nothing more than a concrete representation of the unavoidable reality that I will soon be forced to accept that nothing is impervious to time—not tooth enamel, or marriage, or the perspective that everything will be okay—no matter how entrenched my denial is. Then, the shiny metal instrument touches what feels like an open nerve, and my body jumps.

A shock of pain runs from my mouth to the toes. I issue a whimper as involuntary as the sweat that dampens my armpits and the back of my hair. She pokes around, touches various teeth, and each point of contact makes me cling to the armrests, like a child, as the same shocks of pain run through me. I am desperate to flee and visualize an escape route; jumping out of the chair, down the hallway that smells like antiseptic, through the waiting room, and onto Queen Street. The muscles in my legs are tensing and I'm ready to go; Dr. Nashid pulls out her tiny silver spear and pushes away the bright white light. I remember to breathe.

"There is a lot to do in there. A root canal, I fear. Some gum surgery. Many cavities, five, maybe six. We'll have to take pictures first to know the truth. But all those must wait. First we must get the wisdom tooth out before, ah... before things get worse."

She could not have said anything more terrifying. Her words rip the tenuous seams of my self-worth. I am not flying the X-1. I am not sitting not in the pilot's seat, but in a dentist's chair, and the reality that I'm currently experiencing far more fear than Chuck Yeager ever felt at the controls of his experimental airplane drenches me with shame. This anxiety makes me wish I were a completely different person, while at the same time confirming my darkest fear that I'm not strong enough, not man enough, to become anything other than the puddle of failure slumped into this fake leather chair.

"Should we set up an appointment so I can come back and you can pull the wisdom tooth?"

"No," Dr. Nashid says. She turns the overhead light back on. "We'll have to do it now."

Monica continues failing to ask Ted questions, unable to make eye contact or complete sentences. When she does manage to implicate a verb around an object and subject, her construction makes it a statement, not a question. All she'd really have to do is raise her voice at the end of her sentences, but she's too flustered to even succeed at a task that simple.

"I wasn't fully in my senses."

"Are you asking me if you were?"

"No. It's just that..."

"Your Honour," Diane says.

Justice Royal nods, acknowledging that certain rules are absolute and must be followed, while simultaneously raising his eyebrows, gesture as judgment that makes Diane fall silent. "Monica, I wonder if you might want to go into the witness box. I think you might just want to tell your story."

"I'm so sorry. I'm messing up the procedures."

"Not at all. You're doing fine. Would you have an objection to that?"

"No, your Honour."

Ted steps down from the witness box. Monica takes his place. Her hands tremble as she gets sworn in. It is not a pleasant tale she tells. It starts with a description of the injuries suffered after she was run over by a car: a concussion, compound fractures in both arms and her left leg, torn rotator cuff. The car that hurt her was driven by the father of her newborn child. He'd just pushed her out of it. Body and spirit broken, with a newborn to take care of, Monica went to her doctor, who prescribed a heavy dose of opiate-based painkillers. She was under the influence of this medication when she signed the agreement with Mutual Benefits. She believed that the form Ted put in front of her gave him permission to investigate the legitimacy of her claim. She did not understand that it also gave him permission to go forward with it. Over the next three months, as she was trying to nurse her newborn child, sleeping in a sequence of friends' apartments, single and alone, no fewer than nine different representatives of Mutual Benefits called her. Each time, she explained her circumstances to the representatives, who called as early as eight in the morning and as late as ten at night. Finally, she'd had enough of them, and told them that she wanted the case dropped.

"They never told me that I had to follow up with a letter, that the 'no' I gave them over the phone wasn't enough. That it had to be in writing. Nobody told me that." Monica looks down at the short grey carpet and nods to indicate that she's told her story to the best of her ability.

Diane stands, quickly. She tents her fingers on the surface of her long wooden table and leans forward, a bull preparing to charge. It's clear that mercy is not among her objectives.

"Did you sign a contract with Mutual Benefits?"

"Let me explain…"

"Did you?"

"I signed a form but…"

"Is that a yes?"

"I didn't know, or it was never made clear …"

"Is this the paperwork you signed?"

"It is."

"Is this your signature?"

"It is."

"Did you receive a disability refund from Canada Revenue Agency?"

"I did, but..."

"Did you submit the application for that refund?"

"I didn't want you to."

"Did you?"

"Did I what? I'm sorry. What are you asking?"

"Did you submit an application for a refund from Canada Revenue Agency?"

"No."

"Did we?"

"Yes."

"No further questions."

The needle must penetrate a nerve. I attempt to prepare for this by choosing the most relaxing music I have on my phone, Brian Eno's *Music for Airports*.

"Are you ready?" Dr. Nashid's voice is calm.

I nod, lie back, cover my ears with my headphones, and close my eyes. The music I've picked is too calm, the distance between what I'm hearing and feeling too vast, a gulf that my nervousness fills with the anticipation of pain. Squinting against the clinical light, I wave my hands while trying not to look at the needle, which is much larger than I thought it would be.

"I just need different music."

"That is fine. What are you thinking? Adele? Adele is good."

The needle is silver. The part that will be pushed into a living nerve is three centimetres long. It is impossible to ignore this reality. In fact, it is all I can think about as I scroll through my phone, not knowing what to pick, since there is no *Music for Dentists*. Eventually, I settle on an eighties playlist, because I need something soothing that doesn't sound soothing and I'm hoping nostalgia will provide this.

"You ready?"

Keeping my eyes closed, I return my headphones to my ears. I nod, then open my mouth indecently. Dr. Nashid touches my lower gum with a Q-tip, as if she's making a bull's eye inside my mouth. That area of my mouth goes numb, and I consider, in a rush of self-esteem produced by the thrill of conquering my fears, the possibility that this might not be so bad after all. I am just riding the wave of this feeling, as the Bunnymen continue bringing on their dancing horses, when the needle pierces. It is an electric, searing distress, a sustained intrusive pain. It is much worse than I had possibly imagined. The needle goes in further. The pain increases. My fists clench. My muscles tighten. I am a fish hooked and I dare not move until the needle is extracted.

"I'm sorry. So sorry to do that."

"Blardon?" I pull down my headphones, allowing Echo and the Bunnymen to leak into the small clinical room. I can't seem to uncurl my fingers.

"So sorry. So sorry to do that to you."

"Of dorce."

I reapply my headphones. The dental assistant mops my brow. Her eyes express maternal concern from above her papery blue mask. My shirt is wet. My heart is scared. There is nothing I can say. I close my eyes. Dr. Nashid taps my shoulder, and I slip the left side of my headphones from my ear, but my eyes remain closed.

"I will have to do some drilling before we pull. Are you okay? Can you continue?"

"Of dorce."

"Then we continue."

Her gloved hand gently pushes my mouth further open. Something metallic knocks against a tooth, making me jump. The insect buzz of the drill enters my ears through my teeth. I can't feel my lower jaw. My heart won't slow down. My tongue is a piece of meat in my mouth, frozen. At least the needle has worked, the freezing has taken effect. The timbre of the drill changes as it intersects with my tooth. The drill reverberates. I feel no pain. And then I do—a sharp stab, like someone's touched a broken bone.

"Waid! Stup!"

The drill is turned off. The room is quiet. I open my eyes, and Dr. Nashid tugs down her mask.

"You can feel that?"

"Yeth."

"Much pain?"

"Yeth."

"Your adrenaline! You're having too much adrenaline. It's making your system go faster, burning the freezing away."

"Do you have to try again?" I am suffused with fear, waiting for her answer.

Dr. Nashid pulls off her white plastic gloves. She rolls on her stool to her desk, picks up a pen, and begins writing.

"Here's what we'll do. We will set up an appointment for tomorrow. You come back, we will pull the tooth. But I give you this..." Dr. Nashid hands me the top page from the small rectangular pad of paper. "You take two of these, under the tongue, half an hour before you arrive. It will make you calm. Then we can pull the tooth. Okay?"

I nod and I pull my damp shirt from my chest. My hair is soaked, but it's okay. It will all be over in twenty-fours, I tell myself, but when I go to make the next appointment, the pretty dental hygienist tells me there isn't an appointment available for three days.

"Let's hear summations," Justice Royal says.

As Diane stands up, I do, too. The tips of her sharp fingernails are assessing which tab to select as I bow in the general direction of Justice Royal, then turn my back and use a quick pace to reach the door. I wish Justice Royal luck. I respect him. I can feel the compassion and empathy he has for Monica. He seems like an honest, educated, fair individual, the kind of person I truly would want to be hearing a case like this one. Still, I cannot hear his verdict. The light behind the down button has burnt out so it's impossible to know if the elevator is aware of how badly I need it to arrive. I repeatedly jab the button, as if there's a certain number of times it must be hit before the elevator magically appears. I'm in no hurry. I have nowhere to be. I'm just afraid of the verdict. They have a signed contract, a professional lawyer, legal precedent. All Monica has is sorrow and tragedy and moral superiority. This does not seem like nearly enough. It doesn't even seem like a fair fight. I'm not sure I could face a verdict that didn't go in her favour right now. I don't think I could witness such undeniable evidence that we've set up our society to reward the strong and punish the weak, and continue living in it. The elevator arrives. The doors open. It's too crowded to hold even one more person, and I push my way in.

In Chapter Two of my literary disasterpiece, Simon drives around with Ást, just two green-skinned fellows trucking through Northern Ontario, for three days. Riveting! Exactly what they're doing for these three days is unclear. There isn't any dialogue in Chapter Two, none at all. This is not only absurd for its complete and utter failure to be entertaining in a narrative sense, it's simply wrong. You can drive from Toronto to the Manitoba border in twenty-five hours. So, quite literally, Chapter Two of *Forgive Us Our Eccentricities as We Forgive the Eccentricities of Others* features the main characters driving around in circles.

So little happens in chapters three, four, and five that I'm surprised there wasn't a Brechtian mutiny, that my characters weren't provoked by such a profound state of boredom they simply refused to continue being part of this story. There is, however, one part in Chapter Six that doesn't suck. Ást drives Simon toward an apple orchard, somewhere near the Manitoban border—again, the location isn't specifically mapped out because I guess I thought that leaving things unclear would somehow make it arty, or possibly because I was trying to skirt around the issue that there aren't any orchards in Northern Ontario, because the climate would make such an agricultural undertaking impossible—take your pick. Nonetheless, that's where our two green-skinned heroes go, to an orchard run by your typical guru character mixed with a liberal dose of circus ringmaster.

Ást introduces Simon to Wazzä, who reluctantly agrees to take the young frogling under his wing. From here the book degenerates into a sort of faux-religious writing, a mixture of cat posters and the training sequences found in kung fu movies, as Wazzä gives Simon a series of vaguely Eastern metaphorical tasks to perform. Think Taoism, but in eighties music-video form, cheap and instant. However, before any of that can happen, Wazzä, driving a golf cart— honestly, I have no idea what compelled me to make him drive a golf cart or what I thought that would reveal about Wazzä's character— gives Simon a lift to the cottage where he'll live for the remainder of his stay at the orchard. I kinda like this bit from the end of Chapter Six...

I had not fully sat down before Wazzä drove off into the orchard. This was no grid pattern of trees. They grew in clumps, standing together like co-workers gone out for a smoke. Red apples grew beside green apples, and trees with yellow apples grew a little further down. Some trees were very old and some were quite young. And below all of this, winding through and around these trees, was the most complicated sequence of trails I have ever seen.

Every twenty metres the path forked, then forked again twenty metres later, a web of dirt spun by a jokester spider. I had no idea how Wazzä was finding his way. I just trusted that he was. After some time, the golf cart skidded to a stop. Wazzä put his hands over his eyes to shield them from a sun that had already set.

"Are you lost?" I asked.

"Not yet." The electric motor whined as Wazzä drove up to the next fork. "Which way?"

"I don't know!"

"Choose!"

"I don't know where we're going!"

"Choose! Choose! Choose!"

"Left!"

Wazzä turned left.

"Choose!" Wazzä demanded as we neared the next fork.

"I have no idea!"

"Choose!"

"Right!"

He went right. At the next fork he did it again.

"Choose!"

"Straight!"

"Nice!"

For twenty-five minutes, maybe longer, Wazzä yelled for me to choose, and I screamed a random direction. Then, the sky now blue-black dark, Wazzä stopped the cart, and looked around.

"Finally! I have no idea where we are. We are completely lost."

Without waiting for my response, Wazzä drove forward. Three minutes later, we crested a hill at the bottom of which a small cozy cottage sat on the edge of a six-acre pond.

"How did you do that?" I asked.

"Getting lost is the only way I know of getting found."

Mr. Harrison, the silver-haired plaintiff, stands so erect he's leaning slightly backward, a posture he maintains with such authority it makes the rest of the world seem crooked. He represents himself. The defendant, Michael, sits behind the wooden table on the left, wearing a neutral expression so extreme he appears to be hiding a tiny crime, like standing mid-line in the express aisle with fourteen items instead of twelve. Michael's shoes, suit, and tie are all new and age-appropriately fashionable. His hair looks storm-proof. He appears to be the kind of man to whom flight attendants automatically give a window seat, a gesture he no doubt always fails to appreciate. He continues staring straight ahead as Kevin, his lawyer, stands.

Kevin commands the attention of the court by tugging the French cuffs of his crisp white shirt a quarter inch past the sleeves of his grey woollen jacket. He looks directly at Mr. Harrison and smiles the smile of the initiated. This is not a smile designed to express friendship, but member-ship in a club so secret you and I aren't aware we've been excluded from it.

"Good afternoon, Mr. Harrison. Before I begin, I'd just like to say that I, obviously, am aware of your work and reputation. Your legacy. Although the circumstances are unfortunate, it is a pleasure to finally meet you." This may be the first time anyone in small claims court has taken the time to begin their cross-examination with a compliment. Kevin keeps on with the superlatives, turning his hands in a circle, like gears in a compliment-generating machine. Mr. Harrison does not resist these adjectives. He nods, executes a slight bow each time Kevin uses a phrase like "very senior," or "much respected," or "greatly distinguished." Somewhere around the three-minute mark, Justice Underwood crosses her arms over her chest and tucks her thumbs into her armpits, making her robed forearms look like wings. Her dark eyebrows arch above the thick black frame of her glasses. She has become birdlike, an owl shocked to find herself indoors, in daylight.

"You don't have to apologize for cross-examining him," she says.

"That being said"—Kevin adjusts his tie fine silk and smooths out the bottom of his jacket—"I'd just like it to be known that..."

"We all understand that you respect your elders, but this isn't a job interview. Is it?"

"No. Of course not."

"Then let's get on with this."

"Of course." Kevin clears his throat, looks down at his notes, and hands Mr. Harrison a single piece of white paper. "Please read this email sent on August 20, 2011. Was it sent by you?"

"Yes. I sent that email."

I have a primal desire to believe everything Mr. Harrison's deeply confident voice says. I know that who I think Mr. Harrison is doesn't really exist. I'm aware how much I'm projecting into him. How could anyone eliminate decades of post-modern thought and re-establish the modernist notion of absolute truth with the utterance of a single declarative sentence? However, I'm so desperate for someone who can turn back the philosophical clock that I'm willing to believe, at least for now, that Mr. Harrison is capable of anything. Just the timbre of his voice is enough to evaporate doubt, to bring certainty and objective truth into daily life, leaving no room for anyone to question, or even merely suspect, that his point of view isn't intrinsically accurate. It's a con job pure and simple, but one that's so perfectly performed, so seductive in the black-and-white view of the world it presents, that even Kevin is falling for it. Although, to his credit, he manages to continue his cross-examination.

On August 20, Mr. Harrison sent Michael an email. In it, Mr. Harrison stated that Michael owed him $11,866 for services rendered and offered to reduce the outstanding amount to $5,000. However—and this is the point on which the entire case rests— five weeks earlier, Michael sent Mr. Harrison a cheque for $5,000. Although Mr. Harrison admits to receiving and cashing this cheque, he forgot to include that money when listing the payments Michael had already made. So, no one disputes that these are the facts in the case, but while Michael claims that the July cheque makes them square, Mr. Harrison thinks he's still owed another $5,000. This is a straightforward case that rests entirely on interpretation, a reality complicated by the fact that Michael, Kevin, and Mr. Harrison are all lawyers. This is a trial where a lawyer, represented by a lawyer, is suing a lawyer for lawyer's fees. And the final ruling will be made by Justice Underwood, who before becoming a judge, was a lawyer.

Today is Tuesday. I'm in my second week of coming to small claims court. Out of all of those mornings, today is the only day Jenny has taken my hand. Shortly after her brother rounded the corner and went out of sight, I felt a tug at my sleeve, looked down, and saw her open palm waiting for me to grasp. It felt good to have her hand in mine. She gripped it tightly, which meant there was something important she wanted to tell me, some newly discovered fact she needed to make me aware of. I couldn't wait to hear what it was, but I knew enough to remain silent, that any inquiry into the nature of her concern would scatter her ability to talk about it. So I did nothing but shorten my stride, ensuring that there would be as many steps as possible between where we were and the corner.

I waited for Jenny to say something, but she remained silent. It was garbage day and the large wheeled bins stood on the sidewalk, forcing us to serpentine around them like they were obstacles in a game show. We passed the yard where the Portuguese woman sets out fig trees in large terra-cotta pots, available for sale at $25 each. We walked in front of the house where a small brown dog stood on the back of the couch in the window, barking. Jenny didn't notice any of these things. She walked with her head down. She was lost in thought. Soon we'd reached the house on the corner sur-rounded by the white iron fence and all the flowers, which meant we were running out of steps.

"I want to be a radio singer."

Her voice was small. Her eyes studied the sidewalk. Mine did, too. Shaw Street was less than three steps away, and I still hadn't responded. Jenny's grip became tighter, as if applying enough force could push an answer out of my mouth, like moving air around a balloon. But we contin-ued walking in silence, and I mentally ran through various scenarios, contemplated and calculated the different ways I could respond to her statement. Every possible answer felt pat, or easy, or an echo of wisdom someone had given me that'd turned out to be wrong. I couldn't think of what to say and I had three steps to figure it out.

≈

Kevin keeps returning to the wording of the August 20 email, presenting arguments for his interpretation of Mr. Harrison's offer, pointing to this detail or that phrase. I judge him harshly, consider him petty and manipulative, until I realize that his strategy is my own. Case in point: the descriptions I've presented. I told you Kevin's tie was silk, but I didn't mention that it's slightly frayed at the bottom. I've said that Mr. Harrison has good posture, but I haven't told you that the age spots on his hands and cheeks make him seem frail and old. I've given details and bits of dialogue that increase Justice Underwood's authority, but I've left out the part where she's asked Kevin to slow down and speak louder, which embarrassed all of us, this symbol of authority having a hearing problem.

All the details I've presented are real, authentic, and factual. But each has been selected to serve a purpose, to create an impression, to subtly encourage you to see the conflict in a certain light, to support my interpretation of the events. It's all put together to share my point of view, which I've presented as if it were the truth. This is exactly what Kevin is doing. What all the people in this room are doing. What everybody everywhere is doing. It is perhaps why words were invented: to give us the power to use facts in the service of our own perspective, then to try to convince someone else—a justice, a reader, a lover—to share that point of view. To see it the way we want them to. The vast majority of a human life is spent trying to construct a convincing story. And while it can be argued that this, on occasion, involves telling the truth, it's certainly different from giving the whole story.

What I wanted to tell Jenny, what I'd always promised myself I would tell her when I found myself in this parental situation, is the following: I love your singing and I will support it in every way I can, but the chances of your voice making you enough money to live on, or even channelling significant praise and recognition toward you, are extraordinarily slim. But when I looked at Jenny, steeled myself to tell her these things, I saw so much optimism gushing out of her eyes, along with joy and certainty and a belief in the world as a just place where dreams are goals you have to work hard to achieve, I couldn't do it.

And that, I realized, is how it happens. It's why I believed that my books would be read and cherished by millions, that I would end up sitting in a room being paid to write a world-altering work of literary fiction instead of a manual for the Morris T4-Automatic Dishwasher. All my disappointment in my writing career, my inability to appreciate what I have instead of what I don't, is the direct result of the fact that my parents loved me. They loved me too much to smother my dreams beneath the bleach-scented pillow of realism. Just like I love my daughter too much to rip her treasured aspirations out of her heart, toss them to the sidewalk, and grind them into the concrete with the heel of my boot, as if I were extinguishing a cigarette.

I do not make a lot of money. I cannot frame a house, or drive a car in a snowstorm without fear, or fix simple machines. I am not a fighter. If confronted by a man with a gun, I would encourage my wife to hand over her purse. If our family came across a bear in the woods, I would tell them to run, and then I would run, too. Because it's stupid to risk your life for forty bucks and an iPhone. Because, outside of the movies, no one fights a bear and wins. I wish I had handyman skills, but the truth is I can cheaply hire someone to do a much better job than any amateur could. For the last forty-odd years, not conforming to the lumberjack notions of masculinity seemed not only logical, but subversive. I was okay with defining my own version of manliness because I knew truth to be a relative thing, flexible and malleable. I was strong and confident enough to come up with my own definition of gender, to create a version of male that I felt to be true for me.

But I'm tired. Nothing else has changed—I still know that the notion of absolute truth is bullshit, or at least that truth isn't something firm and consistent that can be carved into stone tablets and raised aloft, that truth can be created, won or lost, by the phrasing of a sentence or the conviction with which it's uttered. In this urbanized, capitalistic world, where we select gender expectations like items at a buffet, balancing an ineptness at auto mechanics with the doing of laundry, setting your personal definition of gender is pretty much a requirement. But lately, I'm just too exhausted to sustain this perspective. I have begun longing for a return to the status quo, circa 1950, or at least the pop-culture version of it. I've become exhausted by the constant need to build the truth.

These days, it's easier to simply conform. I have begun nurturing the ability to accept gender stereotyping, to accept all aspects of social conditioning, from parental expectations right on down to what T-shirt to wear on Saturday afternoons. I'm too tired to fight and, in the absence of my own criteria, I've begun using traditional expectations against which to measure myself. Even though I'm perfectly aware these call for skills I can't be expected to have and for me to form conclusions I could never authentically make, I feel not only that my masculinity is suspect, but that it has been for decades. So now, my core response to my identity as a man is to see myself as someone failing to live up to expectations I don't believe in. I am no longer able to commit to the small claims to subversion I was capable of through my thirties and early forties. Most of the time, this is simply because I'm too tired to confidently venture beyond the white-fenced yard of my social conditioning. But sometimes, as in that moment with Jenny, it's because there are times as a parent when you don't get the luxury of doing what you know is right.

"I think that's great! I think you'll make a fantastic radio singer!" I told her. My tongue ran along the jagged edge of my broken tooth. Jenny beamed. Her grip on my hand became looser, less needy. She was so happy that I began to wonder if everything I believed and held dear wasn't wrong. After all, lying to her, my moment of wilful manipulation, had ultimately created a greater good. So perhaps all my lefty political ideas, all this striving to become a better person, doing my part to shoulder the endless burden of making the world a better place, is stupid after all. We skipped around the corner, and it seemed obvious to me that my friends and I had it right back in high school, that we should do whatever made us feel good, that the yoke of responsibility must be shrugged. The path forward seemed clear and easy. I skipped along beside my daughter. We rounded the corner so quickly that we even caught up to Jack. The three of us crossed Shaw Street together. I felt that despite my rotten tooth, despite the trouble Julie and I were having, despite my mounting sense of professional disappointment, somehow everything was going to be okay.

Then the school bell rang. I looked at my phone. We were

running late, very late, and I hadn't even noticed. Late is something Jack does not like to be. Taking Jenny's hand, he pulled her toward the school and glanced briefly over his shoulder, giving me a look that expressed his disappointed, that said, *How could you do this? How could you let this happen? It's your job to keep us safe, and you've failed.*

"In July, he paid five thousand. That wasn't accounted for, was it?"

"I've said that."

"So you admit to receiving that payment?"

"I was looking for a further payment."

"No further questions." Kevin piles up his papers, folds his hands on top of them.

Mr. Harrison leaves the witness stand, returns to the far right end of his long wooden table. Justice Underwood asks for summations. In ninety seconds, Mr. Harrison acknowledges that the mistake was his, apologizes for it, then repeats that the language of the email clearly anticipates future payment. Kevin uses four minutes to say, basically, hey: a deal's a deal.

"If Mr. Harrison made an oversight, the result of an honest mistake, that would make your version of the truth little more than a financial opportunity. If this is the result of an honest mistake, should he be held to it?" Justice Underwood waits for Kevin to respond. The pause is lengthy.

"Yes."

"So…it's his tough luck?"

"Yes?"

Justice Underwood nods. "Let's take a recess. Ten minutes. Come back at…1:15."

She disappears into her chambers. Justice Underwood is

the only one who leaves the courtroom. Men and women waiting to become plaintiffs and defendants talk amongst themselves. The court reporter flirts with the bailiff. When Justice Underwood returns to her elevated position behind the bench, she looks so refreshed I assume that the main purpose of the recess was so she could pee.

"Judgment for the plaintiff," she says.

Neither the defendant nor the plaintiff seem disappointed, relieved, or happy. Kevin and Mr. Harrison turn, present hands to each other, and clasp with hearty strength. Both are careful to establish and maintain eye contact. Kevin looks away first, and order is re-established.

I guess I should be happy, since I was cheering for Mr. Harrison. But in my heart it feels wrong, as if the truth, after centuries of versatile flexibility, has finally been pushed too far, given up any pretext of resistance, submitted fully to our will. I can see it lying there on the courtroom floor, defeated, floundering beneath the bright clinical fluorescent lights, the absence of shadows portraying its submissive posture with pure, unflinching detail. *Do with me what you will*, truth whispers as it lies on the short fibres of the grey carpeting. *You were going to, anyway.*

11. FORGIVE US OUR ECCENTRICITIES AS WE FORGIVE THE ECCENTRICITIES OF OTHERS: PART THREE

Simon stays at the orchard for three or four weeks. I've skipped ahead eleven chapters, and yet I'm able to summarize what you've missed in a single-clause sentence. We're now on page seventy-six of the manuscript. There is nothing worthy of saving in all of these pages, except, possibly, this scene from the end of Chapter Fourteen.

Simon's on the verge of having had enough, thinks Wazzä's just dicking him around. You've seen this a thousand times before. It's *that* scene. Simon has packed his bags with anger, he's holding back tears, blah, blah, blah, storming away in a youthful huff of rage, when Wazzä appears out of nowhere.

And yes, I have Wazzä driving around in the fucking golf cart again. Also, I've previously failed to mention that one of Simon's biggest problems is that he has an inexplicable fear of water. Isn't that brilliant! A giant talking frog who can't get wet!

Enjoy...

> As I stormed away, I heard the familiar yet unwelcome sound of Wazzä's golf cart. He came toward me, slowing to match my pace.
> "I will give you a ride," Wazzä said.
> "You don't have to."
> "Come on. Hop in."
> It seemed rude not to accept his invitation of assistance. Especially since I'd convinced myself so firmly that I had to go. He now had power over me—there was nothing more he could take

from me, no more insult that would stick. I got in. We passed a pond that I hadn't noticed before. Wazzä drove me down to the water's edge.

"How's the pond look?"

"It looks like it wants to kill me."

"What about those?" Wazzä pointed to a bunch of sticks just to the right of the water.

"Those are much less threatening."

"Good." Wazzä then pointed to the surface of the pond and handed me a Zippo lighter. "I want you to take this lighter and those sticks and start a fire underwater." Wazzä crossed his arms over his chest.

"I'm afraid of the water."

"Really?"

"Don't do that."

"Must have forgotten." Wazzä raised his eyebrows like a bank teller in front of a gun.

"But also—that's impossible."

"Is it?"

There was something about Wazzä's phrasing, some sense of certainty and mystery, that got to me. I wanted to continue my exit, but I found I could not. I got out of the golf cart. I took the Zippo and carried the sticks down to the water's edge. It took me several hours, but I finally put my hands under the water. Then, I tried to build a fire beneath the surface. I tried many different ways. I tried lighting the sticks above water, then bringing them down. I grouped the sticks into a teepee, lit the top, then blew on the flames to encourage them as they dipped below the waterline. I tried more desperate techniques. I spent the whole day doing this, alone. The sun was setting when I heard the electric whine of Wazzä's golf cart as he pulled up and parked beside me. Once again, I was filled with a frustration bordering on rage.

"I can't do it! Nobody can make a fire underwater."

"I agree."

"Then why did you make me try?"

"Because it is essential to learn that some things are impossible."

12. ANZIGITY

The directions tell me to, "PLACE 1 UNDER TONGUE LET DISSOLVE BEFORE SWALLOWING." Such bad writing. Why remove the *your* between *under* and *tongue*? The *pill* between *let dissolve*? Whose tongue? What should dissolve? To save eleven characters they've eliminated an exponential amount of clarity. But what do I care? The pills are small and blue and I've already taken three. A streetcar goes by Dr. Nashid's office, rattling the windows, producing what seems to be a symphony of rumble, and I realize the benzodiazepine has already taken effect.

There is no sense of transcendence, no enlightened insight or rush of self-confidence, but even without any of these properties, I can tell you that benzodiazepine is the drug I've been looking for all of my life. The pills have not only removed my anxiety, they've washed away any residue, removed even trace amounts, made me so free of it that I could confidently hand over my passport and attempt to cross the border into the state of self-assuredness. This elimination of worry has made me realize how much worry I routinely carry, like the loudness of a construction site revealed at quitting time. Could the majority of the world really feel this good most of the time? Are there men and women walking around this full of security? Feeling this safe? I feel slightly resentful, thinking about everything I could accomplish without the invisible vultures of anxiety continually perched on my shoulders.

I'm still revelling in this potential, knowing that there are at least seventeen more pieces of magic in the translucent yellow white-capped container, when Dr. Nashid comes into the waiting room. She sits down beside me. She spends a few moments looking directly into my eyes.

"How are you feeling today?"

"Fantastic!"

"Are you sure?"

"Absolutely."

"You've taken the medication?"

"Yes!"

"So you feel that you are ready?"

"Let's do this!"

Dr. Nashid doesn't laugh at my enthusiasm, just leads me down the overlit corridor into the small, windowless room. The instruments gleam on their silver tray. The capped needle makes a forty-five-degree angle across the manila folder that bears my name. Blissed on benzodiazepine, I feel no fear when I see these things. I know my fear is there, but it's in a cage, sleeping in the corner of the room. As the pretty dental assistant ties the blue paper bib around my neck some behind-the-camera part of me, for reasons that are still unknown, prompts me to snap my fingers.

"So. You are ready. Then if you could lie down, please?"

I do. Dr. Nashid pushes my mouth a little wider open. She dabs my lower left gum with a Q-tip. The needle still prompts me to close my eyes. It hurts. I breathe deeply. I picture my heart beating slowly. Then I can't feel the needle anymore. I open my eyes. A sequence of large steel instruments goes into my mouth. The drill sounds. And then, using a surprisingly consumer-grade pair of pliers, Dr. Nashid reaches into my mouth. It's almost through sound that I feel the ends of the pliers grasp my tooth. She begins to pull. Dr. Nashid tugs harder. I can feel my wisdom tooth resist, then begin moving, pulled out of its socket and through my flesh. It isn't painful. Not even metaphorically. My mind conjures no allegory for the trials of acquiring wisdom itself. I just sit there, eyes open, focusing on the feeling of the tooth, which is no longer part of me, moving through the flesh that still is. I close my eyes as well. I listen to the sound of water running. Sometime later, the pretty dental assistant taps my shoulder.

"Here you go," she says, and hands me a clear plastic container, the kind that would come filled with ketchup alongside a takeout hamburger. Inside it is my wisdom tooth. I can see the tooth's jagged edge, the rough patch my tongue loved so much. I sit in the chair, grinning, shaking the plastic container, examining the tooth's unexpected size as it rattles around, some sort of rare specimen, a butterfly captured in a faraway climate and brought home to study. This is when the words of a woman I saw earlier that morning, in the hallway outside of courtroom 313, come back to me. She was a strange, frail creature in her early twenties wearing too much mascara. Her black roots had grown three centimetres into her platinum hair. Her fingernails were bitten. Her shoulders were hunched. All of these things combined to create the impression that her spirit animal was a raccoon, although she radiated not impish confidence but worry and anxiety. She spoke in a quiet, husky voice that I heard only because I was walking past her.

"When I'm scared, it's hard for me to believe that anybody knows what to do more than I do," she said.

I will never know the context in which these words were uttered. The man she spoke to could have been her lawyer or her social worker, but based on the way the two of them were conspiratorially huddled together on the hallway's only bench, how their fingers reached out toward each other but did not touch, I'd say they were in the very preliminary stages of becoming more than friends. He caught me staring at them and then led the raccoon girl farther down the hallway, where they continued their now-animated discussion by the elevators.

Her phrase stayed with me as I took the pills and got into a taxi. And as Dr. Nashid finishes packing my mouth with gauze, I feel a desperate need to say them out loud, as if the phrase is an oath or a spell, something that must be spoken out loud for its power to fully take effect.

"When I'vm scared it'z 'ard fer me to bulieve anzone znows what to do butther thzn I do," I whisper.

"What's that?" Dr. Nashid asks. I hadn't meant her to hear me. But now that she has, encouraged by the continuing effects of three hundred milligrams of benzodiazepine, I feel a desire to explain myself.

"Zan I hell you sumting?"

"Are you being frightened?"

"No. I vant to hell you hhy I'm zo frighzed by denizry, luve, zyah fuzure."

"You're having a good day if you can tell me that."

"Whin I'm szared it'z 'ard fer me to bulieve anybody nows wuat to do butter than I do. Tis da root of my anzigity. Makes me gate convol—even if it's somethin I now nothung aboat. Meh fear iz zo shrong zat I half to do somethig. I gate convol! The ting iz, sumtizes I shold gate control. Nd sumtizes I sholdnt. But I dnt mate zat dezizion based on facks but anzigity."

"Of course."

I shake the plastic container. The wisdom tooth rattles. Dr. Nashid and the pretty dental assistant are eager to attend to their next patient. I know that. I have no desire to stay in this windowless room. But still I seem unable to convince myself to go. I continue sitting, giggling slightly because the idea that dental surgery has just changed my life seems very strange to me.

Justice Olivetti tilts back her tiny grey head and stares at the flickering fluorescent lights on the left side of courtroom 317. The bailiff, a tall, thin man several years beyond the age of retirement, stands at the back of the room with his hand on the light switch.

"Flick it now," Justice Olivetti calls.

The bailiff flicks the lights, off and on, several times. The plaintiff, Alex, a middle-aged man in a white shirt so new that the folds from the packaging are visible, is already in the courtroom. So is the defendant, Sarah, a middle-aged woman with red hair, whose fist holds a lipstick-stained tissue. They both crane their necks backwards, looking up as if they're expecting rain.

"That's enough."

The bailiff stops flicking the lights. The long tubes illuminate fully. The flickering has ceased.

"Much better." Justice Olivetti looks down at the defendant and the plaintiff and smiles broadly. It is a smile that neither Alex nor Sarah is able to return.

Today I woke up with my son's eyes, bright and green, less than three inches from my face. His entire head floated above me like some divine embodiment, a minor god from the cosmology of a culture I'd never heard of. I had to look up at him, which was a perspective neither of us had ever experienced before. Jack's head tilted to the left, as if he were encountering a mystery. The sunlight came through the front windows, revealing how badly they were in need of washing. My neck was stiff from the unnatural position in which I'd slept, and my face was sore from the rough texture of the white canvas covering the Ikea couch.

"How long have you been there?"

"Why are you on the couch?"

"I fell asleep watching TV."

Jack looked over his shoulder, saw that the screen was black. His eyes became filled with a skepticism beyond his years. "Then why isn't it on?"

"I turned it off."

"While you were sleeping?"

"Do you want breakfast?"

"Is this your bed now?"

"Waffles? Syrup?"

"Yes!"

"How many witnesses?" Justice Olivetti asks the defendant.

"Just her," Alex says. He points a .22 calibre finger to his right, directly at Sarah. He continues pointing at Sarah long after these words have left his mouth. It should be noted that at no time has Alex made eye contact with Sarah, that he seems unable to even turn his head in her general direction. Sarah looks down at the thin grey carpet like she's scared of the walls.

Justice Olivetti takes all of this in and releases a sigh that ruffles her bangs. "Then call her."

Sarah takes the stand, gets sworn in. Her hair falls in front of her face as she looks at her folded hands. With a slowness employed in the hope of producing a dramatic effect, the plaintiff raises his head and, for the first time, looks at the defendant. There is a pause. He continues to stare. The clock hums.

"Use your words, Mr. Bert." Justice Olivetti leans back in her chair and crosses her arms.

"I'm waiting for her to look at me."

"She's not required to look at you. She only has to answer your questions."

Alex runs his hand through his thinning hair, straightens his tie, which doesn't need straightening, and buttons the top button on his jacket. All these gestures combine to form a note-perfect imitation of every television lawyer about to question a hostile witness and win the big case. "Were we married?"

Sarah looks from her hands to Justice Olivetti.

"It's a valid question," Justice Olivetti says.

"Yes."

"For how long?"

"Six years."

"At 173 Russet Place?"

"You know this ..."

"Yes or no?"

"Yes."

"Until?"

"Until what? The day?"

"That's what I asked..." Alex's voice is patronizing, scolding, getting louder. The construction of his question asks for information, but the tone asks for a fight. Sarah drops her gaze back to her folded hands. What I took for being meek and submissive might actually be an attempt to avoid getting sucked in.

"September."

"That's when we were divorced."

"It is."

"I asked you when you moved out."

"Wednesday, October 14." Her voice is suddenly proud, and there's a significance given to the way she pronounces this date, as if it were the birthday of a national hero or the end date of a long war that had ravaged both sides. Sarah looks up from her hands. She stares at Alex. He looks away first.

At breakfast, everything appeared to be fine. I made coffee. Julie came down in her housecoat. I made waffles. We went through the beats of a familiar morning: coffee, conversation, CBC Radio. We were respectful with each other. Our words were gently spoken. When I forgot that the kids needed to go to dance class tonight, we simply adjusted our plans. None of these triggers, these small things that we'd usually stretch and pull until they were large enough to carry our resentment and disappointment, set us off. There was no fighting, no name-calling or accusations, no turned backs and bitter silences—and that's exactly what frightened me.

It would have been easy to see this as a turning point, the moment we set all our resentments on fire, pushed them into the water, then stood on shore watching them burn. But it didn't feel like that. The absence of anger left a vacuum that wasn't filled by happiness, but a sort of low-grade despondency. There was no warm hug, no kiss at the door when I left to walk the kids to school. The absence of hatred didn't allow love to reign, disappointment didn't twist itself inside out and become joy. There were no transformations at all, just a slow-moving sadness that coated my heart with one more thick, toxic, tarlike layer of remorse and regret. Because it wasn't that Julie and I had agreed to stop fighting, or even postpone it: fighting just wasn't important enough to commit our limited energies to. It was simply something we no longer cared enough to do.

≈

For fifteen minutes, Alex asks Sarah questions composed of equal parts accusation and insinuation, and it soon becomes obvious that the justice Alex is hoping to extract isn't monetary, but emotional. Although he is suing for $6,723—the calculated total of items Sarah kept in a storage locker that he claims were never disclosed when they agreed to the terms of their divorce—what Alex really wants is a judgment confirming that Sarah was wrong to leave him. He'd prefer this ruling come from Justice Olivetti, since she's the highest authority in the room. But based on the number of times he turns and looks at those sitting in the gallery and the heavy dramatic length of his pauses, any of us will do.

And then again, maybe we won't. As Alex's questions continue, he seems to forget all about us. He forgets about the bailiff and the court reporter and even Justice Olivetti. He tunes out the humming clock and the fluorescent lighting that has once again started flickering. There's only one person he cares about, only one he wants to convince, and she's in the witness box. Sarah answers all of Alex's questions with simple declarative sentences, often one word long. Twice, she's paused and looked over at Justice Olivetti to make sure she has to answer a question that seems particularly irrelevant, but this is the closest she's come to cracking. Sarah has presented a demeanour so emotionless that Alex has been unable to find a way in; she's a cliff made of glass, impossible to climb. Clearly Alex's strategy is to wear her down, but it's having the opposite effect. With each monosyllabic response Sarah gives, a little more exasperation comes into Alex's voice, not hers.

"In our settlement, were we not to divide our property equally?"

"Yes."

"Do you feel like we did that?"

"Yes."

"Honestly?"

"Move on, Mr. Bert."

"What about... Don't you think... Aren't there certain items in your possession that aren't in mine?"

"No."

"That belong not just to you?"

"No."

"Aren't some things worth more than money?"

"Yes?"

"Do you also agree that the things you got were worth more than money?"

"What are you asking, Alex?"

"You got things that were worth more emotionally!"

"Just tell me what you mean, Alex."

Sarah says this calmly. Her shoulders relax and the tension leaves her face. There is a glimmer of what is unmistakably love on her face. She's keeping it in check, but the look is there and Alex can see it. I can only assume the sight of this is painful for Alex. The look on her face reveals that at one point she really did love him. But it also has the feel of a ghost, something that used to be present but no longer is, an expression constructed from shards after the biggest pieces have been swept up, placed into an empty cereal box, and tossed away.

"The photo album! I want the photo album!" His sudden anger is both shocking and expected, cliché.

"I scanned all of those pictures. I printed them out. I gave them to you. The digital files, too."

"That's not enough! I deserve the originals!"

"Mr. Bert, I believe you're through with your question-ing." Justice Olivetti pivots in her chair and looks directly at the plaintiff.

"I have a couple more."

"Do they open new and relevant areas of investigation?"

"Yes."

"Do they?"

"Yes!"

"Are you sure, Mr. Bert? I want you to be very, very sure."

Alex looks up at Sarah. He sees that her smile, as small and fleeting as it was, is gone. For several moments he is still and the courtroom is quiet.

"No. No they won't," he finally says.

This is the problem with our perception of love. We're told that real love is indestructible. The other side of this thought is the conclusion that any love that isn't forever isn't real. It's not true, but most of us believe it. So when a relationship comes to its natural conclusion, as so many of them are intrinsically structured to do, we don't know what to do. We sit there, knowing in our hearts that the love we felt was real. But we also know, with just as much certainty, that the love is gone. These two thoughts cannot be simultaneously held. This is why it's so hard to let go of a relationship that's ended—if we do, it means it wasn't love in the first place.

It is no surprise when Justice Olivetti decides in the defen-dant's favour. She asks for the next case. Sarah quickly leaves the courtroom, her hands tucked into the ends of her sleeves. Alex watches her go. He does not return his notes to his backpack as the court reporter calls the next case and he's pushed out of the way.

I go home. I write these notes. I kiss my sleeping children. I pack a bag and write a note. My cab will arrive in ten to fifteen minutes.

PART THREE

LIONIZED

14. SPELLING LESSONS

There was a pattern in the carpet, wheat sheaves embroidered in golden thread, that I followed, foot over foot, arms extended like a high-wire artist, all the way to the front desk. The sound of a vacuum cleaner came from the mezzanine. The operator remained out of sight. The slender ivy-leaf hands of the large, elegant clock in the middle of the lobby said it was 2:17. I put my hands on the white marble counter, which was cold. There was nobody behind it. A sequence of nature photographs saved the computer's screen. Sesame seeds rested inside the yellow paper that a fast-food bagel had come wrapped in. White stringy headphones lay beside the computer like something aquatic found on a beach, stranded and dead.

There was no bell to ring. Six minutes passed—a figure I know to be exact because I repeatedly, compulsively, checked the time on the large clock behind me, and then a young woman returned to her post. Her name tag said *Brenda*. Her pupils were gigantic. She smelled like skunk. Jiggling the mouse, Brenda brought the computer back to life. She checked for email, her phone for texts, and after confirming she'd received no new messages, Brenda turned her attention to me.

"How can we help you?"

I contemplated the many ways I could answer this question. The first that came to mind was tossing my hastily packed suitcase into the air, jabbing my index finger toward the elegant clock, and asking her what *she* thought *I* wanted. Another option was to let this be the moment I broke down, the moment I let all of the sadness and fear pour out of me, to cease resisting my ever-increasing sense of feeling unsafe and finally collapse into a weepy puddle of middle-age failure on the embroidered carpet beneath my scuffed leather dress shoes. It occurred to me that the opposite approach was available, too, that I could repeatedly raise and lower my eyebrows, slap my credit card on the marble countertop, and make innuendo-soaked comments that strongly imply a passionate devotion to decadence and vice, behaviour that would culminate in whichever king-sized bed she assigned me. What I actually said surprised us both.

"Forgive my eccentricities as I forgive the eccentricities of others."

"Excuse me?"

The vacuum from the mezzanine stopped running. The sound of traffic leaked through the rotating doors. I closed my eyes to enjoy the stillness. When I opened them, Brenda was checking her phone.

"A room. I just need a room."

"For one night?"

"Yes. Possibly more."

Inside the elevator, the button for the twelfth floor lit up as I pressed it. The doors closed, making a mechanical clatter rarely heard in the digital world. I found it soothing. The elevator began to rise, and something about this motion, so slow and smooth with a clear end in sight, triggered the understanding that I was in the middle of a mid-life crisis. I was doing my best to pretend that I wasn't having one, but clearly that's what's happening to me. And there, in between the third and four floor, it became clear that my mid-life crisis is not the result of dwindling power and limited opportunities, but of sincerely questioning whether I want to keep fighting. Whether the consequences of continuing to strive, both mentally and physically, are sustainable or desirable. A mid-life crisis isn't provoked by an inability to move upward, or the realization that long-held goals are no longer attainable, but from questioning whether fighting to achieve them is worth it. That the destination I've spent my whole life travelling toward may not actually be a city I want to visit, let alone a place where I want to hold the mortgage on a five-bedroom, three-bathroom detached with a nice backyard. And standing behind this difficult realization, eager to gain my attention, was an even bigger one: that my goals were never worth it in the first place.

The elevator continued upward. I remained the only one in it. It was somewhere between the seventh and eighth floor that I lost all hope. I'm not saying that right then and there, as the overhead indicator lights flashed their predicable sequence, I made the decision to type "tie a noose with curtains" or "ways of breaking unbreakable glass" into Google. But for the first time in my life, suicide seemed pragmatic. As the elevator rose, I felt an extraordinary pressure, self-produced and even more insistent for it, to make a decision how I was going to react to this urge before I arrived at my floor.

When the doors opened on the twelfth floor, I knew that the only course of action available to me was my old friend procrastination. So I continued down the hallway and slid the plastic card into the door marked 1207. The lock clicked open. The small room was filled with furniture that had been mass-produced to give the feel of hand-crafted antiques: a writing desk, a wardrobe, a king-sized bed. I stood in the hallway, looking in. When the door grew too heavy to keep holding open, I took my suitcase with me into the bathroom, and from it I retrieved the translucent yellow pill bottle.

The lighting in the bathroom made me squint. I avoided eye contact with the mirror. My intentions were to take a single pill, but it did not take long to realize that this was a metaphoric task, which, if achieved, would have mythic ramifications provoking ironic punishment. It was a dilemma: one pill would eliminate my anxiety, but once the bottle was open, there would be no taking just one pill. So I didn't open the bottle. I had a long bath. I tried to get myself off but I couldn't conjure a fantasy, and the overpriced high-production-value pornography available through the in-room entertainment system was so choreographed that actual penetration seemed stagy and fake. The room felt very small. I had to leave it. I rode the elevator up and down for half an hour, until the motion made me seasick. Wobbly, trying to regain my balance, I walked through the silent, Brenda-less lobby. Outside it was cold and I could see my breath. I widened my stance, tipped my head backward, and breathed in and out, watching thin white clouds leak out of my body. I closed my eyes. I listened to the city until I wasn't dizzy anymore. It was too quiet. The abandoned streets felt unsafe, and I twirled through the circular door, back inside.

Returning to my room, I inspected the emptiness inside every drawer, then had a second bath. I dried myself off. I tossed the towel onto the floor. It fell into the shape of a P. Crouching down, I took the towel and shaped it into an L. With the addition of a washcloth, I made an E. I continued to do this, making letters, using the same towel and washcloth to shape an A, an S, another E. I made an L, an E, a T in sequence. I continued until I'd formed the phrase "please let me sleep," a silent plea to an absent god, heliographs carved not in of rock but from linens scented with lemon.

Whether superstition or answered prayer, it was in this moment that I finally began to feel sleepy. I closed the curtains, pulled the comforter off the bed, and collapsed face down on the mattress. I was exhausted but still awake minutes later when the sun started to rise. I turned my head and stared at the white wall to the right of the curtains, watching the colours shift and change as more and more light crept around the heavy fabric. When the room was filled with that optimistic yellow light only sunrises provide, I managed to fall asleep.

I'm underground, standing on the King subway platform, waiting for the northbound train, when the relative emptiness makes me realize it's Saturday. Small claims court is closed on the weekends. I have no technical writing to do, since the Howlstein Corporation still thinks I'm on vacation. I cannot go home. The sixteen hours between the present moment and two this morning—a time when I'll finally, possibly, feel tired enough to attempt falling asleep—seems like a sentence, run-on and incoherent. I leave the subway. I get coffee. I look at records in records stores. I go to the Art Gallery of Ontario and stare at million-dollar paintings. It's not even noon. It really isn't a surprise when I find myself returning to the wedding chapel at Toronto City Hall.

Using the *Globe and Mail* cover story again, I approach various wedding parties, but they're more interested in privacy than publicity. Then, just before 2:30, I catch the attention of a mid-twenties bride and her groom as they step out of the elevator, and deliver my pitch. The sequins covering the bride's gown and the tiara in her hair make it seem like she's wearing a costume, not a wedding dress. He's dressed in grey denim jeans and a white turtleneck sweater. Their faces express interest: raised on celebrity-gossip websites and reality television, they are clearly taken with the idea of their nuptials receiving media coverage.

"You just want to...what? Be there?" the bride asks.

"I'll stay at the back. Keep perfectly quiet. Just taking notes."

"I'm okay with it," the groom answers.

"Cool with me, too," the bride says.

The elevator doors open behind her. The rest of their wedding party step out. As the party moves into the wedding chapel's foray, they seem to have already forgotten about me.

Time is succinctly measured at the city hall wedding chapel. On busy days like Saturdays, weddings are performed sequentially, one right after the other, in half-hour intervals. A wedding had just concluded when Andrea and her party came into the chapel. Another one is scheduled to begin in sixteen minutes. This is why I'm surprised that at 2:42, even though twelve of their thirty minutes have been spent, the ceremony has not begun, let alone concluded. The groom is outside, smoking. There are four other people in the wedding chapel accompanying the bride: a bridesmaid, the bridesmaid's boyfriend, the bride's mother, and a bald, quiet man who has a tendency to stand a little back from the action, leading me to assume he's the mother's second husband. The bride, Andrea, speaks in a loud hush as she continues talking on the phone. The officiant, whose short silver hair, thick black eyebrows, and long black gown create the impression of an affable crow, points a remote at the stereo, changing the New Age spa music to Mozart in harpsichord. Then, he approaches Andrea, smiles reassuringly, and hovers until she feels obligated to lower her phone.

"Is everything all right?"

"It will be."

"We'll need to start the next ceremony at three."

"I understand."

"Are you waiting for someone?"

"My fiancé," Andrea says.

The officiant nods, walks away. But Andrea's bridesmaid, Pam, who wears a green low-cut dress that in no way matches the bride's, isn't buying it. She knows that David, the groom, is merely outside having a cigarette, retrievable at a moment's notice. Pam whispers something to her date, a tall, stocky man with unnerving pleasantness, who might be cast in a frat-house comedy as a character named Moose, then she joins Andrea in the middle of the room.

"What's wrong?" Pam asks.

"I texted them to go to city hall."

"Okay?"

"They went to the one in Brampton."

"Oh. That's bad. But if the next one starts at three…"

"She has his ring."

"Yours or his?"

"His. His dad's. The one I'm supposed to give him. I didn't want to lose it, so I gave it to Stephanie."

"Fuck."

"I know."

"They'll get here."

"They're on the Gardiner."

"It's important?"

"It's an heirloom. It's crazy important to him. It has to be the family ring."

"Then they'll get here. It'll work out," Pam says, although she does not look convinced.

Last night I missed my kids, so I called Julie. The phone rang six times and then Jenny answered.

"Daddy!"

"Hey, baby. How are you?"

"Great."

"How was your day?"

"Great."

125

"What did you do today?"

"Stuff."

"What kind of stuff?"

She sounded farther away than sixteen city blocks, stranded on the other side of everything that stands between me and her mother, all the unsaid and oversaid things currently making it impossible for me to return home. The phone call was having the opposite of its desired effect, making me miss her and her brother more than not talking to her would have. My heart was breaking a little bit, and so I began looking for ways to end the call as quickly as possible, like a pilot in a malfunctioning aircraft desperate for a runway.

"But you're good?"

"I'm great!"

"Okay. Good. Let me talk to your brother."

"Jacccck," Jenny called in a loud and confident voice. The phone slips from her hand, and for a brief moment it's not just the phone that's falling but me as well. Only it doesn't feel like a downward motion but a falling upward, a floating, like a helium balloon accidentally released from someone's grip, suddenly free but doomed to keep rising until atmospheric pressure causes it to pop.

It's 2:47 when the groom, having just consumed what he assumed would be his last cigarette as a bachelor, walks back into the wedding chamber. He's visibly nervous, his large Adam's apple bouncing up and down as he takes Andrea's hands.

"Let's do this," David says.

Andrea looks at her phone, sees that there are no new messages, and suggests that they take pictures. Documentia takes over as everyone, bride and groom included, pulls out their phones. They hand their phones to each other and take various group shots. Soon it's 2:51 and guests for the 3:00 have already started gathering outside the wedding chamber. Waiting is no longer an option.

"If we do this fast, we can still have you leaving here as husband and wife." The officiant's voice is loud and attracts everyone's attention. He stands at the front of the chapel, waving for David and Andrea to move toward him. They do. Pam and Moose, mother and stepdad, move too. The officiant steps forward, begins. He goes straight to the vows, which are standard, asking Andrea and David to unite in good health and bad, for richer or poorer, until death does them part. These are the same vows you've heard in movies and sitcoms and that they're David and Andrea's choice makes me question their sincerity. It doesn't help that the bride and groom are trying to stifle giggles, that no one is crying or has noticed that the CD player is on repeat and "Ave Verum Corpus" is playing in a loop. I don't know why these two decided to get married. I suspect it is from need instead of want, that this ceremony is solving some problem, either practical or emotional, which is why it's being held here at city hall, and why the bride's dress is a little too frilly and the groom's attire is a little too casual.

I'm about to paint this entire ceremony in Cynical Black when David reaches up and touches Andrea's cheek with the outer edge of his index finger. The touch is light. It lasts only a second. But it's enough to kindle a transformation, forcing the bride and groom to almost accidentally look into each other's eyes, where they find a sincerity that surprises them both, an unexpected burst of authentic emotion that burns away all the kitsch, collapses the ironic distance, turns camp into heartfelt emotion. Unfortunately, it isn't enough to provoke a miracle. The wedding chapel doors do not burst open. Stephanie remains on the Gardiner.

"With this ring, do you take David to be your lawfully wedded husband?" the officiant asks. From the front left pocket of his jeans, David pulls out a silver wedding band. He has trusted this ring only to himself. Unlike the ring Andrea was in charge of, which currently sits inside a car stuck in traffic many miles away. David's eyes well up as he slips the ring on Andrea's finger.

"And now for the bride," the officiant says. Andrea looks at the floor. Her posture tells all of us that she has ruined everything. She begins to cry. Her mother steps toward her. There is whispering between them.

"No?"

Andrea does more whispering.

"Really?"

"I don't know what to do."

"Why don't you use mine?" the mother of the bride says. The bride and groom are motionless, silent. The clock continues ticking. The next wedding party can be heard assembling in the foyer. The officiant raises his bushy eyebrows.

"That's weird, Mom," Andrea says.

But her mother is already tugging her ring off her finger. It gets a little stuck at the knuckle, and she's forced to wet her skin with her lips, then pull and pull, the intrinsic slapstick comedy of this gesture provoking laughter from everyone in the room. Finally freed, she hands the ring to her daughter, who nods and says nothing so her tears won't turn into sobs.

This is the best introductory lesson on how to be married that I have ever witnessed. It is what marriage is. As far as I know, there are very few moments in any marriage in which things go as planned. In my experience, marriage is about nothing other than winging it, going forward even though there's no solution in sight. Marriage is about having the faith to do this. It's about knowing that success will never, ever, come in the form you pictured it would, yet will contain elements far surpassing it. Andrea pushes the ring onto David's finger. It won't go past his knuckle. This causes both of them to laugh. With her right hand, Sarah holds the ring in place. She holds it tightly.

"I now pronounce you husband and wife," the officiant says.

The couple lean toward each other, kiss. Then they kiss a little deeper. Andrea wraps her entire hand around David's finger, which she holds tightly, which she will not let go of.

"Where are you?" Jack says.

"I'm in a hotel."

"Why are you there?"

"I'm working."

"Mom says you're taking a vacation."

"It's a working vacation. Did you finish that Lego thing?"

"Yah."

"How'd it turn out?"

"Good."

"Can you send me a picture of it?"

"Are you coming home?"

It's his phrasing that stops me cold. Perhaps it was just an accident, the result of the mere ten years he's been forming sentences, but the distinct lack of qualifiers in his questions makes me suddenly feel like I'm falling again. He did not ask me when. He asked me if.

"Soon."

"Honest?"

"Honestly. Two or three days, tops. I promise you. I just have a couple more things that I have to get done."

"Okay. You want to talk to Mom?"

"Sure."

"Mom..."

I hear Julie walk closer to the phone. The phone gets transferred between their hands. I want to tell her that I love her, that we can work this out, that we'll find a way to make everything like it used to be, that I want to keep going forward with her. But all I hear is silence, and then the line goes dead.

16. FORGIVE US OUR ECCENTRICITIES AS WE FORGIVE THE ECCENTRICITIES OF OTHERS: PART FOUR

This is the best passage in all of *Forgive Us Our Eccentricities as We Forgive the Eccentricities of Others*. It is the only part of the book that I still consider publishable. I think maybe I'll try to write it as a short story. Or maybe just save it to slip into something new I haven't even started yet. But the point, what I'm saying, all I'm saying, is that even in the massive misstep of a manuscript there are glimpses of beauty.

Although I still can't believe the fucking golf cart.

Wazzä reached inside the cooler and pulled out an apple. It did not seem to merit the sense of occasion Wazzä commanded to introduce it.

"What do you think?"

"It's a nice apple."

"Look closer."

I looked closer, yet remained unmoved.

"Look at it!"

"I'm looking!"

"It's the perfect apple!"

"Is it?"

"The shade, the shape, the texture, the degree of ripeness—look at the way it just folds into my hand! Finding an apple this perfect isn't just a matter of aesthetic appreciation, of having the eye. No! You have to actually be able to see not just the apple, but the future. This apple will remain perfect until...maybe noon? By evening, it won't be perfect anymore. Do you understand? Such a slippery target, perfection! This apple, as perfect as it is, will only be so for the next three or four hours. It will only be the answer until lunchtime, tops."

Wazzä bit into the apple, the resulting crunch almost as loud as the previous night's frogs. Still chewing, he took a second mouthful and then a third.

"Today you have to find your perfect apple."

I got out of his golf cart. He drove away. At the top of the hill, Wazzä tossed the apple away, half-eaten.

Without hesitation I crawled into the cottage, stuffed what little I'd unpacked back into my knapsack, and once again I stormed out of the orchard. I did not have time to waste on meaningless bullshit like hunting for goddamn apples! My head down, my pack digging into my shoulders, I followed the most recent golf cart-tracks in the dirt trail, stomping my heel onto every apple that my foot came near. Although I tried not to, a part of me couldn't stop comparing each apple my boot squished into the dirt to the one that Wazzä had just called perfect. I was unable to stop rating the various shades of red, the degree to which their shapes were toothlike, how much each one resisted the downward motion of my boot.

That's all it took. First, I took off my pack. An hour later, I'd carried my pack back to the cottage. The rest of the morning I searched the ground. In the afternoon, I started climbing trees. For twelve hours, I looked for an apple that matched the one Wazzä had shown me. I didn't find it, not even something close. I slept well that night. I got up early. I spent the next day searching for an apple just like Wazzä's. I spent three days searching that orchard, obsessed.

On the morning of the fourth day, I came out of the cottage, my back sore from searching the ground, my arms aching from climbing trees, the ends of my fingertips sandpapered raw from gripping bark. The golf cart was parked at the east end of the pond.

"How's it going?" Wazzä asked.

"I can't find it." The defeat in my voice was strong. "I can't find an apple that even remotely looks like the one you showed me."

"Is that what you've been doing?"

"That's what you told me to do!"

"All this time? Three days? That's what you've been doing?"

"I've been working hard!"

"What are you, some kind of idiot?"

There just wasn't any good way to respond to that. Wazzä took a cigar out of the inside pocket of his too-tight grey jacket. Using miniature scissors, after several long minutes Wazzä meticulously cut off the end of the cigar. Seemingly oblivious to the implications of the gesture, Wazzä put the cigar in his mouth and coated it with a thin layer of spit. By the time he'd lit the cigar, Wazzä seemed to have forgotten that he'd been on the verge of saying something. But he hadn't. Several puffs later, his eyes went large and he leaned in toward me.

"Don't you realize that the perfect apple for you will look absolutely nothing like the perfect apple for me?"

17. THE CAVALRY ISN'T COMING

At 10:19, eighteen minutes after the recess was supposed to end and the trial was slated to resume, the defendant, Michael, stands, rolls his shoulders in the manner of a boxer, and takes long overconfident strides toward the door of courtroom 310. He wears a black suit. His tie and shirt are both made of silk. Janice, the plaintiff, takes off her clear-rimmed glasses and replaces them with the blacked-rimmed pair that hangs from a chain around her neck. She twists in her chair, just in time to see Michael pull out his cellphone as the door closes behind him. Ninety seconds later, the court reporter comes in and notices that the defendant's chair is empty.

"Where's he gone?" she asks Janice.

"He went to call his wife," Janice says.

"Has he gone *home* to call his wife?" the court reporter says. Janice laughs a little louder than she needs to.

Here's everything you need to get you up to speed on this trial: Michael, the man who has just gone out into the hallway to call his wife, is the manager of the Golden Glow Spa. In 2008, Janice frequented his establishment and received a Botox injection. She claims that Dr. Fountane, the facility's resident doctor, delegated her Botox injection to an employee, a woman who may or may not have been a registered nurse, and that woman botched it. Janice suffered bruises, swelling, and emotional trauma, which is why she's suing the Golden Glow Spa for $25,000, the exact maximum small claims court allows. It should be noted that Janice was also suing Dr. Fountane, but that case has since been dismissed.

Ten minutes pass before Michael comes back into the courtroom. The court reporter steps out, then ushers in

Justice Glidden, a tall woman with perfect posture and long black hair in ringlets, whose practically regal presence captures the attention of everyone in the room. Taking long, graceful steps, she seems to glide to her chair, and we all rise without reluctance. Court resumes. In the previous session, Janice concluded her case. Which leaves Michael preparing to mount his defence, although you wouldn't know it by looking at the empty chairs beside him or the single piece of paper he hands to the court reporter.

"What is this?" Justice Glidden asks.

"My witness isn't coming. I have prepared this affidavit instead."

"You didn't do your research. Court rules demand that such documents be submitted thirty days prior to trial. The court will not accept it. Now, who is this witness?"

"Matilda Swinger."

"What's she to you?"

"She's my wife."

"Your wife?"

"We own the spa together."

"Where's this wife?"

"She's looking after our children."

"At your home?"

"Yes."

"That will not do."

"My apologies."

"She'll have to come down here. She'll have to come down right now."

"She has to tend to our children."

"Then I suggest that she pack a laptop, some movies, headphones, snacks, the kids, and get herself down here." Justice Glidden learns forward in her chair, creating an intimidation factor inversely proportional to her calming grace.

"It's impossible."

"We're going to start at one o'clock. Either way, whether your wife is here or not, you'll be mounting your defence." And then, for the second time today, Justice Glidden puts the court into recess.

Hey.

Yes?

I think we need to talk.

I don't.
It all seems clear to me.

Please?
It's important.

What's the point?

Don't you want to see me grovel?
No grovelling then?
Just talking?
Please?
I've already called my mom.
She's coming over to sit the kids.
She'll be there at 7:30.

What did you tell her?

Nothing.
Just that we need a night out.
Please?
Peter Pan?
8:00?

I'll be there.

It is nine minutes after one when Michael enters courtroom 310 with his witness. He helps Matilda with her coat. Her hair is carefully braided, her clothes are pressed, and her makeup is perfect. It does not look like she was rushed. There are no children in tow. Matilda hands her husband a folded piece of paper from the pocket of her coat. Then she takes the stand, gets sworn in. Her husband unfolds the paper and flattens it out against the surface of the long wooden table. He then begins to read from it, raising his voice at the end so that the statements transform into questions.

"How are you associated with the Golden Glow Spa?"

"I manage it."

"What's your relationship to Dr. Fountane?"

"He rents a space from us."

"So he is not your employee?"

"I am his landlord."

"So are you legally responsible for his actions?"

"Not in any way."

"Thank you," Michael says. He has no further questions. Janice quickly stands, then takes a long dramatic pause. She taps the top of the wooden table in a slow, winding-down rhythm. There is sustained eye contact between Janice and Matilda. Each seems determined not to look away first.

"Where did you purchase your Botox?" Janice asks.

"The doctor does that."

"Who's Jack Alexander?"

"I don't know."

"You told me he was one of the lawyers." Janice's voice is getting louder and higher in pitch.

"I don't know who he is."

"At any time, did I ask for or demand a refund?"

"Yes, you did."

"When?"

"There was a message from Brett. To call you back."

"Do you remember me asking for help? Where should I go?"

"No."

"Do you remember suggesting that I see a doctor? Or see another clinic?"

"No. Not that I recall." Matilda's voice is now as loud and high as Janice's.

"Do you remember banning me from the spa?"

"I remember you harassing, with the calls. Several times."

"How many times is several?"

"Twice that day. And two a day for a week! You were very rude!"

"I'm very insulted that I'm being lied to!"

"Madam!" Justice Glidden says. "I'll determine who's telling the truth."

It's obvious that Matilda is lying. Janice knows it. Michael and Matilda know it. Justice Glidden knows it, too, but adherence to the rules of law means she has to pretend she doesn't. What I'm witnessing is a quintessential example of the depths to which someone will fall in order to avoid admitting the truth, simply to win a victory, to keep from admitting they were wrong. No amount of energy, passion, confusion, or humility will be spared in these efforts. Even when our lie has been made obvious and everyone around us knows that we're lying, even when we ourselves are perfectly aware that we're not telling the truth, our default setting is to continue spinning facts and reinventing history. There is only one reason that could make us do all of this: the fear of losing love. I will do anything, absolutely anything, to keep from losing love.

I am beginning to fear that this makes me unlovable.

Janice takes a deep breath, slowly pushes it out. Her legal strategy seems to have rested entirely on cracking the witness, trying to break her down, elicit a big confession. But that's a strategy that only works on TV. Janice takes off her glasses, sets the black-framed ones beside the clear-rimmed ones.

"I don't...I don't have anything more," Janice says.

Matilda, still on the stand, twists so that her back is to the justice. Facing her husband, she winks.

When I arrive, Julie is already there. The tables are mostly empty. A waitress leans on the bar, checking her phone. Julie sits at the table by the window, drinking red wine from a long-stemmed glass. I walk toward her, wondering how to manifest a greeting through physicality—a hug will be awkward, a kiss on the cheek too formal. There is no physical expression for the space we currently occupy, no agreed-upon gesture to convey that we are currently neither lovers nor friends, though we are husband and wife. So I just sit down, put the napkin over my lap, and turn in my chair, seeing if I can find the waiter's attention.

"I would have ordered you something, but I wasn't sure what you'd want."

"It won't be the peppercorn steak."

Julie does not laugh. The waiter arrives. I order a beer. I regret this choice. I worry that I've disappointed Julie by this, that I should have ordered something classier, a Manhattan or a sidecar. The waiter returns, sets down menus. I open mine and find myself unable to make sense of the sentences. I'm reading the words, but my brain is running too fast to transform them into information. I realize it was a mistake not to have taken a little yellow pill.

"Thank you for coming," I say.

"We have some things to work out."

This phrase makes me begin falling again, or floating upward, it's difficult to tell which this is. I fear that we're over, finally and forever beyond repair, that she's here simply to demonstrate she can be, that she will be, civil, straightforward, but she's already made the decision to leave me. I continue to fall/float, so shaken by the prospect of future years of split Christmases and long lonely nights spent in rooms illuminated by the bluish flicker of an unwatched television that I am suddenly not only able but compelled to speak from the heart. Although, it is in a rambling, barely coherent way.

"Before, last week, maybe two weeks ago? God, I'm not even sure anymore. But you asked me why I was angry all the time. I didn't give you an answer. I still don't have one, not really, not a firm elevator pitch, not a well-constructed sentiment, a logical sequence explaining it all. But I have this, and this is all that I have. These are the things I can admit to. I know that a lot of this, my moods, my unhappiness, my quickness to anger, to take trivial, meaningless disagreements and transform them into opportunities to vent the frustration that continually boils, like lava, inside of me, is because of the distance between where I am and where I thought I would be. That my failure to live up to what could very possibly be my unrealistic expectations have made me sad and pathetic, have left me weak and whiny and troubled, and I am unable to see anything but the gap, the lack, the infinite list of what I don't have, and I am unable to see the finite but very real, tangible, solid things I do.

"I also acknowledge: who would want to fuck that? Who could possibly find that sexy? Who could possibly sustain love based on the flimsy memory of its existence a decade ago, for the person I used to be? Who could live in continual hope that somehow something will fan the quickly diminishing embers and you will find a way to love again? No one can. I realize that where I am, in my current state, makes me impossible to love. And that now, now that you've seen me like this, the memory of this version of me will be impossible to unsee. I realize this. I acknowledge this. That you see this side of me so often that you've come to believe it's all I am. And I get it—who would want to let that into their heart? I accept this. I know this is true. But I'm still so angry that you don't even try!

"Is my love for you the same as when we met? No. It isn't. But the love between us is sixteen years old now. It doesn't demand the same sort of intensity from us anymore. Does that mean it's as strong? As powerful? I'm not sure. I really don't know anymore. But I'm willing to try to figure it out. I want to try to figure it out with you."

Having finished, I put my hands on the table, very close to hers. It is easy for me to picture my heart sitting beside them, just to the right of the candles, beating quickly, staining the white tablecloth with its leaking red messiness. I feel proud of my rant, that I've finally articulated what our problem is. Then I look up at Julie, see the distance between her eyebrows and her eyelids, and it's clear that she does not agree.

"That's not our problem at all."

"It isn't?"

"Our problem is that we believe there's a solution. The cavalry isn't coming. We are not en route: we have arrived. None of these problems will ever be fixed. This is it. This is us. This is who we will always be. Either accept it, get on board with it, or don't."

I am rendered silent. Not because her words have made me too angry, shocked, or fearful to reply, but because they need no improvement.

"Are you coming home?"

"I... Soon."

"Can you pick up the kids on Friday?"

"Of course."

"Don't forget about Friday?"

"I won't."

Julie stands up, puts on her coat, then walks to my side of the table and bends down. I turn my head so she can kiss my cheek. She kisses me, deeply, on the lips instead.

18. LIONIZED

The benches in the hallway outside courtroom 311 are short and constructed from a material that sounds like plastic when I strike it with my fist, but feels like steel to the touch. Whatever this space-age substance is, benches should not be made of it. This is the most uncomfortable bench I have ever sat on. This stretch of hallway is overheated. The fluorescent lighting is excessive. All of these things work together to create a passageway so uncomfortable the effect must be intentional: it is an interior engineered to stop you from lingering, to keep you moving along. At one end of the hall is Hazel, and at the other is Mary. The two women have put as much space between them as the hallway allows.

Hazel is slightly younger. Her eyes are rimmed in black and she wears a skirt that would be too short for court if she weren't wearing thick tights. Mary wears nylons and a black dress that would be suitable for either a cocktail party or funeral. The lock on the door to the courtroom clicks. The court reporter opens the door from the inside and kicks a rubber stopper underneath to prop it open. We all go in. To my surprise, Hazel sits behind the long wooden table marked *Plaintiff*, Mary behind *Defendant*. Justice Smith enters and Hazel and Mary, for the first time, do something together as they rise in unison.

Last night, Karl Ove Knausgård was in town. The great Norwegian realist was being interviewed by Sheila Heti at the Drake Hotel. There was a time when Sheila and I enjoyed an equal level of literary fame. Both our first books were published by small presses and received positive if tentative reviews peppered with the phrases like "great potential" and "writer to watch." We were both occasionally invited to be panellists on CBC Radio programs and appear at fundraisers.

But then Sheila just exploded all over the place. Her collection of short stories was picked up by a prestigious American press. Her first novel was published by an even more prestigious American press. But it was her third book, a semi-autobiographical coming-of-age story with a sex-positive feminist twist that really broke things open for her. International sales, tours, all of it culminating in a feature profile in the *New Yorker*. Now she writes for the *Paris Review* and *Granta*, spends a lot of time in New York and gets flown to Australia for readings.

Yes, obviously I was jealous. Worse than that, I was envious—it didn't seem fair that Sheila was getting all this glory, living the life I not only dreamed of, but firmly expected to have, the life I believed I deserved. The problem is that she's a really good writer. Her prose is original, unforced, and honest. Admittedly, she is a distinctive voice worthy of recognition, but what really made her success hard to take was how it hadn't gone to her head. If anything, Sheila's fame has made her more relaxed, less pretentious, left with nothing to prove.

It had been a while since we'd seen each other, but I decided to go to the interview. What else was I going to do? The prospect of spending the evening praying to a higher power by shaping sentences out of the linen was unappealing. I took a shower, used the iron in the closet to press my shirt, and closed the door of my hotel room firmly behind me.

Mary has stopped pretending not to stare at Hazel, although the look of scorn she's sending her way cannot be considered an improvement. Hazel calls her only witness, and Betty, a middle-aged woman who'd be good cast as the nosy neighbour in an American sitcom, gets sworn in.

"Who do you work for?"

"Devil Girl Home Furnishing."

"What do you do there?"

"I work in the credit department."

"What is the nature of that work in the credit department?"

"I collect on unpaid loans."

"If you could read the highlighted passage?" Hazel hands Betty a piece of paper. Betty reads the highlighted passage, a clause so indecipherable that even in my capacity as a lowly technical writer, I'm offended. Justice Smith asks for clarification and it's eventually revealed that two and a half years ago Mary went on an epic shopping spree at Devil Girl Home Furnishing, store #117, located at the corner of Bloor and Bathurst, where she basically outfitted the entire first floor of her house. She bought two couches, a love seat, end tables, six kitchen chairs, and a new refrigerator. All of which she bought on credit that was approved and financed by Devil Girl Home Furnishing's own in-house credit operation. For the first year, everything was fine. In the second Mary fell behind on her payments, then stopped paying altogether. Devil Girl Home Furnishing is suing for $17,321, the original purchase price of the furniture plus incurred interest.

These things established, Hazel closes the brief. She has no further questions.

"What's the interest rate?" Justice Smith asks.

"Seven percent," Hazel answers.

"For the full term?"

"For the first twelve months, yes."

"And after that?"

"Twenty-seven-point-eight percent."

"I see."

The courtroom is quiet for a while. Betty remains on the stand, and Marvin, whose suit and organizational skills both appear rumpled, bursts into the room, apologizes for his lateness, and begins his cross. By his own admission, Marvin only received this case a couple of hours ago and hasn't really had time to fully look it over. He does what he can, asks a bunch of obvious questions, solicits information from Betty that she's already freely put forth. When Marvin has no further questions, Hazel rests her case.

Marvin mounts his defence, which seems to consist exclusively of asking Mary to take the stand.

"Can you state your name?" Marvin asks.

"Mary."

"Are you married?"

"No."

"Divorced?"

"Yes." Mary's voice is cold and her monosyllabic answers give the impression that she's answering questions from an opposing lawyer, not her own.

"Kids?" Marvin looks down at the paper open in front of him. He seems slightly surprised by what he sees.

"Yes. I have two."

"Very good. Okay..."

Marvin asks three more questions before Mary begins taking the lead, finding places to explain that she's a single mom with two kids who thought she'd hit it big when she got a job as an assistant accountant with a production company. This is what led to the splurge on furnishings. But then she lost her job when the dollar went up and the U.S. productions stopped coming north to shoot. She hit tough times, made tougher when the second year of the contract kicked in and her monthly payments more than doubled from interest alone. Mary negotiated a settlement agreement with Devil Girl Home Furnishing, who agreed to lower the amount owed and gave her a repayment structure. But part of this deal was a clause that, should Mary miss a payment, her debt would revert to the full amount. She honoured five of six payments, but on October 27, the day before the very last payment was due, Mary lost her bank card, which left her unable to make her usual payment. Mary says she explained the situation to a customer service representative named Karen, who told her to just mail a cheque. She directs Marvin, who eventually finds a photocopy of the cheque for $3,500, which he presents into evidence.

This cheque, Mary says, was never cashed—either the bank never put it through or it never arrived. She called Devil Girl Furnishing a couple of times, tried to follow up, got the runaround. In June, she received a letter from the Devil Girl credit department telling her they wanted the full amount, $17,321, Marvin nods, has no further questions. He is not fully seated, but Hazel is already standing, her lips forming the hard consonants of her first question.

Knausgård took long, easy steps as he walked across the stage. He was tall and as good-looking as his author photo promised; his clothes were well tailored and worn in. He greeted Sheila warmly. The stage was as spare as their respective prose, two leather armchairs angled toward each other and a small, clear coffee table, on which sat two bottles of water and Sheila's notes. Knausgård waited for Sheila to sit. His fingers rested calmly in his lap. It was at this moment that I realized I'd come with a disingenuous heart, that I'd wanted to see Knausgård slink onto stage as a frayed wire of nervous energy, with neurosis and anxiety exposing how his brilliance as a writer had destroyed him as a person. But he wasn't like that at all. There was an audio problem, and even before the technician fixed the microphone pinned to his lapel, long before Sheila even asked her first question, the casual arch of his shoulders and the laugh lines around his eyes made it obvious to all he wasn't damaged, not in any way, to any degree.

Knausgård is pretty much the opposite of everything I've turned out to be, the literary Superman to my pop-culture Bizzaro. He writes serious, weighty novels based on his life and has achieved both international literary recognition and best-selling status. I write funny little stories about talking frogs that are marketed as novels even though they're novellas and I'm lucky to sell a couple thousand copies. For all my talk of compassion and empathy, my outstanding ability to feel both, the essential importance of both, I found myself unable to rise to the occasion—every moment Knausgård continued to be self-deprecating, while still managing to maintain his authorial authority, made me a little more bitter and weak and pathetic. I wanted to leave, and just when I'd found a good moment to do so, Sheila caught my eye from the stage, gave me a nod, and smiled in approval at my presence.

So I had to sit there, forced not only to witness Knausgård's greatness but my own inferiority. After the last question was finally asked, I rushed to leave, but the audience was excited—they'd just witnessed something significant and, wanting to savour the moment, they were in no hurry. I got caught up behind a woman on crutches, and when I finally made it out of the auditorium to stand on the sidewalk in the chilly autumn air, my timing couldn't have been worse: less than a foot in front of me, Sheila and Knausgård were climbing into a taxi.

"There you are! Get in here!" Sheila called. She grabbed the shoulder of my jacket and pulled me toward the open door of the taxi. To resist would have revealed how small and petty I am, something I'm too small and petty to do. So I got into the back of the taxi. I sat in the middle of the bench seat, next to Knausgård, Sheila piling in after me. Sheila introduced us, shut the door, and we went east on Queen.

Hazel stops herself, doesn't say anything. Ninety seconds pass. This seems like a very long period of time. Then, without clearing her throat or taking a drink of water, striking like a cobra in a cowboy movie, Hazel asks her first question.

"What date did you say you lost your bank card?" Hazel asks.

"October 27."

"And that's the first date that you attempted to reach Devil Girl?

"Yes."

"When you lost your bank card, what did you do? Did you go into your branch?"

"Yes. I did."

"On what day?"

"I didn't get a chance to go to the bank that day. I have a hard life!"

"I'm not trying to upset you."

"Yes, you are."

"She has a right to ask these questions." Justice Smith says this with a surprising tenderness, then looks back at Hazel and nods for her to continue.

"When did you photocopy this cheque?"

"Just before I mailed it."

"You made a photocopy of the cheque?"

"I photocopy everything."

"When you lost your card, why didn't you use another payment method? Did you try to pay online?"

"I lost my bank card. You can't get on without the number."

"You're meticulous enough to make copies of your cheques, but you don't have a record of your bank card number?"

Mary pauses.

Marvin studies his hands.

Hazel continues, quietly, brutally. The inconsistencies Hazel points out are many. She points out that the number of the photocopied cheque is out of sequence with others Mary wrote that month. She asks why Mary only called Devil Girl twice, because she must have known that the cheque hadn't been cashed, what with the $3,500 sitting in her bank account.

"Is the $3,500 still there?"

"Where?"

"In your bank account."

"No."

"Was it ever?"

"What?"

"Was the money ever there, in your account, in the first place."

"Of course it was!"

"Do you have a photocopy of a bank statement proving this?"

"It's not fair!"

"Do you?"

"You don't get it!"

"I have no further questions."
"I have a hard life!"
"No further questions."
"It's just not fair! It's not fair! It's not fair."

Someone, perhaps three or four passengers previous, has smoked in the taxi, but the smell of tobacco is distant and mixes well with the fall air. The radio is silent. My hands are in my lap, but unquietly so, since this puts them in close proximity to the crotches of both Sheila and Knausgård. But all of these sensory details, the wind coming in the open window, the copy of *Cottage Life* that for some reason is tucked into the pocket of the back of the passenger seat, do not seem nearly as present as the sound of Mary's voice. I can still hear it. Her righteous indignation keeps playing in my mind as I sit between Sheila and Knausgård in the back of this taxi heading east down Queen Street.

It's not fair! It's not fair! It's not fair!

The degree to which Mary's stupidity, her utter lack of personal responsibility, reveals my own suddenly seems like the funniest thing I've ever experienced. Trying to suppress the laughter building up inside me just makes it worse and I am unable to stop a significant giggle from bursting out of me into the excessively uncomfortable quiet of the back seat of this cab.

I have a hard life!

"What?" Sheila is playfully impatient, glad to have something to un-awkward this silence, and I realize that she isn't so cool and calm and collected. She's nervous as well. I may be nervous to be in a taxi with Sheila—but Sheila is nervous to be in a cab with Knausgård.

"What?"

"Nothing!"

"Tell me?"

"Just something I saw in court today. Where are we going?"

"I thought we'd go to the Hyatt bar."

"Yuck. It'll be packed with European tourists. Let's just go to Sweaty Betty's."

"That's a much better idea."

Leaning over me, Sheila pushes her small body into the space between the driver and passenger seats. She gives the cab driver the new coordinates and he makes a sudden U-turn that sends both her and me slamming into Knausgård. There is something about this accidentally forced proximity, an awareness that, regardless of literary merit, we are all still subject to centrifugal force, that chills all three of us out.

Five minutes later, we walk into the Sweaty Betty's, where the pervasive darkness is punctuated by Christmas lights. I enter this establishment flanked not only by Sheila Heti but Knausgård, currently the world's most lauded literary figure. Nobody looks up. He goes unrecognized. Such is the glory of literary fame. The three of us sit at the bar, Knausgård in the middle. We have several drinks. We talk about surviving cold weather and semicolons and how the books we consider our best sell the most poorly, things all three of us have in common. At some point Sheila excuses herself and heads down the stairs to the washroom. When we're alone at the bar, Knausgård leans closer to me.

"Sheila tells me that your books are very good."

"That's kind of her."

He nods at my wedding ring. "You have kids?"

"Ten and eight."

"The best and the worst? I mean, more the best, of course, but you know what I mean?"

"I do."

Knausgård shifts on the bar seat so that his shoulders hunch over. Without moving his head, he looks up at the Christmas lights suspended from the ceiling. He stirs his drink with a red plastic stick shaped like the CN Tower. He starts talking so quietly that it takes several moments before I realize he's talking to me.

"One of the first real conversations I ever had with my daughter—she was maybe three or four and could easily put sentences together, but not always paragraphs—happened while I was driving and she was buckled into her car seat. My mind has deleted where we were going, or coming back from, or why there were just the two of us. These things, which were most important at the time, have now proven themselves to be irrelevant. You know what I mean? Sometimes I think about this, that while I worry about phone bills and deadlines, the detail that will prove itself most significant appears to me as an annoyance. I don't mean to tangent off.

"So, that day she asked a question I didn't really understand, so I turned the rear-view mirror so it reflected her and not the traffic.

'What was that, sweetie?'

'How do I do lion?'

'You want to see a lion? You want to return back to the zoo?'

'No. Be lion. I want to grow and be lion.'

"The conversation continued like this for some time. I wanted to just give up and tell her that I understood what she was saying, even though I didn't. You know how it is?"

"I do."

"Eventually, it became clear that she was asking how

she could turn into a lion. Somewhere, somehow, she had gotten the idea that as she grew, she could become a different animal. That part of growing up was choosing what animal you would become, that growing up didn't mean you'd become a bigger human, but that you could shift species as well as size. Conversely, to her way of thinking, all of us, all the humans around her, were at one time different animals as well. That a turtle, or a horse, or a walrus decided that they wanted to become human when they grew up, and so that's what happened.

'So a lion. I'll do lion, she was telling me from the back seat.'

'Oh, baby. That's a beautiful idea. But it doesn't work like that. What else can I say?'

'No?'

'I'm afraid not. You'll always be a person. You'll just be a bigger one, like me or your mom.'

"My daughter, she begins to cry. She would not stop. She cried until we were almost at our destination, wherever it was, and she'd only stopped because she'd cried herself to sleep."

Here Knausgård pushed a large breath of air past his lips, making what could only be described as a fart sound. He lifted his drink to his mouth and poured what remained inside him.

"Do you know what I mean?" He turned and looked at me. His eyes were blue. His stare was easy.

"Yes. Very recently, but yes."

"Very nice to meet you." Knausgård ignored my protests, took several twenty-dollar bills out of his wallet, and placed them on the bar. When Sheila returned from the bathroom, he was already gone.

The defendants stand behind a polished wooden table at the front of courtroom 301, wearing coats. The room is overly warm. Marie's coat is thick and blue. She's in her forties, frail, running her fingers through her hair, trying to tame it. Ray, her husband, who's acting as her lawyer, is beside her. His coat is red and his hair is grey, stringy, and needs washing. Marie and Ray stand close together. They don't touch. Both their heads jerk to the right as Justice Hermes enters the room.

Justice Hermes has a slight limp, a military haircut and already seems annoyed. He sits down. On the wall behind him, the Royal Crest hangs on an angle, noticeably crooked. He circles his arms to make some room inside his robe, pushes his glasses up to the top of his head, and looks at Marie and Ray. The rules of small claims court, of any court, allow the wearing of suit jackets, but never coats. He doesn't ask the defendants to remove theirs.

"Ready?" he asks.

Marie looks at Ray. Ray nods his head.

"You?" he asks the plaintiffs.

"Yes we are, your Honour," Perry says.

The plaintiffs are also a man-and-woman team, but are so dissimilar from the defendants they seem a sort of scientific opposite. Their clothes are black, fashionable, wrinkle-free. Their hair is recently cut, well-behaved. It's a professional relationship, with Perry in charge. He pulls papers out of a black leather briefcase that looks brand new.

"I have just one witness," Perry says, and nods at Doris beside him. She wears bangs and silver jewellry, and has been sitting to my right, staring blankly ahead, for at least the twenty minutes I've been in this room. Doris strides over to the witness stand, gets sworn in. It is quickly revealed that she works for the debt recovery firm that's hired Perry. He asks short questions. Doris gives precise answers. They've clearly done this before.

Doris's employer, Recovery Premium Management, buys debts that other banks and loan companies have given up on. RPM pays cents on the dollar, then unleashes its collection agents, who do whatever they need to in order to turn that paper into cash. Over the next fifteen minutes, Perry and Doris provide a paper trail proving Marie once had a loan with Morris Investments, which she defaulted on. According to Perry, RPM bought that debt from Morris Investments, and he wants the court to make her pay it.

"A total owing of $5,500," Perry says.

Hearing the figure makes Marie look at the floor.

"Okay." Justice Hermes flips through several of the documents Perry provides. He pulls his glasses down off his head. "Where's the document that proves you own this specific loan?"

Perry pauses. Several moments pass. He produces a document, earlier presented to the clerk, who hands it to Justice Hermes. He looks it over.

"This just proves that RPM bought a bulk of bad debts from Morris Investments. Where's the paper that says you bought her loan?" Justice Hermes asks.

Perry pauses again. This pause is very long. Marie and Ray are the only people in the courtroom who fail to notice this.

"Do we have it?" Perry finally asks Doris.

"No," Doris says. "Maybe I could try again?"

"You have that documentation?" Justice Hermes asks.

"I have no more questions."

Ray starts his cross, mumbles some questions. He does not ask Doris for proof that RPM owns Marie's loan. The rest of his questions go nowhere and then he calls Marie to the stand. She has a French-Canadian accent and is extremely soft-spoken. Justice Hermes asks her to speak louder. She doesn't. He loses his patience, commands her to do so. She looks up, speaks up, angry.

"I took out a loan to buy a car. The car never ran well," she says. Marie explains that shortly after the warranty expired, the engine blew. The car sat in her driveway for the next four years, during which time she was still paying for it, unable to afford to get it fixed.

"Then my husband had a heart attack," she says. Her voice cracks. She can't look at Ray. It's clear that this husband is not the one she lost. With no income, she fell behind on her payments. Morris Investments refused a lower monthly. She defaulted on the loan, sold the car for $200.

"But you did default on the loan?" Justice Hermes asks.

"Yes," Marie admits. She looks back down, leaves the witness stand. There's the distinct impression that this is a woman who hasn't gotten a break since she bought that car, as if the purchase put a curse on her. She's still looking at the floor as she stands beside Ray. Small claims court judges have up to three weeks to render a decision. Justice Hermes does not need this much time. He calls for lunch, and when court returns, he's ready. Ray and Marie, Perry and Doris rise in unison to hear the verdict.

"I see absolutely no evidence before me that the plaintiff has received acquisition of this particular debt. Since the documents are from May, records should be available. The case is dismissed."

At first Marie does not move. It's like she's scared to break a spell. Then her shoulders start to shake. She begins to cry. She tries to cry quietly. She cannot stop. She's still crying when the sound of the next plaintiffs and defendants drowns out the sound of her tears.

I guess the knowledge that I'm walking on a tiny, thin wire, that there is a lethal drop between the bottom of my feet and the ground far below me, was inevitable. In my twenties, it was pure confidence, however unearned, that propelled me forward, and I never paused long enough to look down. I just keep going forward, living life as a series of uninterrupted steps, each one bringing me closer to whatever goal I was chasing in the moment. Then, somewhere in my late thirties, I had my first glimmering realization that failure, that a lack of arrival, is possible. But it was in my forties, after my forward progress had slowed, and the firmness of my conviction in the righteousness of that goal grew soft, that for the first time I looked down.

The act of looking down, this phase of my life forcing me to see the catastrophic consequences of my every misstep, knowing how easily everything can go wrong, the gravity-assisted pace with which failure arrives, has been overwhelming and undermining. None of my usual strategies have worked to resist it. It's not a realization I can fight and defeat. It isn't knowledge that I can forget—I've tried to push it down and each time I do, somehow, in unpredictable ways, it bubbles back up from the depths of my unconscious, madder and meaner for having been repressed.

My age, however, has also given me a weapon, a strategy as unsexy and pedestrian as it is productive: insight gained through failure. Here in middle age, my confidence is no longer the result of naïveté or bravo but repetition and endurance. I've been walking this tightrope for more years than I care to admit. I know how to do this. Knowledge of how high up I am and how easily I can fall, while initially shocking, doesn't actually affect how I put one foot in front of the other. It is at this point, as I sit in the courtroom, tears streaming out of my eyes as quickly as, and perhaps even faster than, those coming from the defendant's, when I realize that once you've looked down, the secret is remembering to look back up.

I go to Canadian Tire. I buy an orange plastic bucket and J Cloths and Pine-Sol and those orange-and-yellow sponges that come in packs of three. I get back into my car. I drive east on the 401. The traffic is light because it's just after noon. I go by feel because I can't remember what number the exit for the gas station was. I park by the pumps, but I don't begin filling up. Finding the key in the glove box, mixed amongst paper napkins and the owner's manual and the last three CDs I will ever own, is harder than finding the gas station itself.

The place is busy. No one notices me. Unlocking the trunk, I take out my bucket and cleaning supplies. I go to the bathroom, fill the bucket with hot water, and begin to scrub. I clean the sink. I wipe off the mirror and the walls. I take a deep breath, then I get down on my hands and knees and clean the toilet. I scrub every corner. I make it as clean and shiny as anything short of a new coat of paint could possible achieve. Then I go back out to my car, put ten dollars in just to get the tank topped off.

When I go inside to pay, I leave the washroom key on the counter.

≈

It was 3:15 when I arrived at their school, which was cutting it close but within acceptable limits, satisfying the promise I'd made to Julie that I'd pick up the kids. All the other mothers and fathers were already there. I stood just back from them, close enough that I wouldn't appear anti-social, but far enough away I wouldn't have to make conversation. Five minutes passed. The bell rang. Hundreds of children poured out of the school, my two kids amongst them. Jenny held my hand, and Jack was at least happy enough to see me that he didn't run ahead. We all arrived on the east side of Shaw Street at the same time. We all looked to the right and all three of us saw the bicyclist. He was coming toward us, quickly. It seemed unlikely that it was the same bicyclist as before. I knew that the odds were very low. But in my mind it was and will always be the same guy, coming south on Shaw at an accelerating speed, displaying the same disregard for two children and their father waiting to cross the street. Jenny's grip on my hand got a little tighter. Jack looked up at me, worried, fearing that the peace and reconciliation of this moment was about to be shattered by rage and anger and a quick reveal of his father's dark side.

But I just stood there. The rage did not return. What I felt instead was concern. Knowing that the cyclist was about to blow through the stop sign, I looked over my shoulder to make sure there wasn't a car coming. And this concern, this compassion, wasn't generated because I'd somehow accepted the bicyclist as one of the things in the world beyond my control. Or because I held Jenny's hand and Jack's attention, so I knew that the bicyclist wasn't a threat. As he came toward us, speeding up instead of slowing down, I was able to see him as just some kid racing somewhere. Maybe he was in a hurry, prompting him to make a bad decision. Maybe he just didn't think it was a big deal if the three of us waited three seconds to let him pass.

All I wanted for this kid was exactly what I wanted for my kids, for my wife, for myself: to be safe. For a brief moment, this is what I wanted for everybody alive. I saw the whole world not as my rival, an adversary for a diminishing pile of resources, but slight variations on the same theme. What we all need, more than riches, or recognition, maybe even more than love, is to feel safe. Then, this feeling was gone. I could remember the construction of the sentiment but not the insight, what it felt like to fully understand it. But that was enough. I watched the bicyclist zoom over the last two metres of pavement between him and the stop sign.

"Be careful. Okay?" I said quietly, as he passed us.

The bicyclist didn't even look over his shoulder. Or maybe he did. I'm not sure. I didn't really check.

"Who wants to go swimming?" I asked.

"We have to do spelling," Jack said.

"I do!" Jenny said.

"Let's go swimming!"

Jenny's hand was in my left and I took Jack's with my right and the three of us crossed Shaw Street together and went back to our house. I packed a suitcase. I packed another for my son and a third for our daughter. We got into the car. They strapped themselves in, and we drove west on Highway 401, past Milton, past Guelph. We kept driving west, eventually stopping at the Stay Awhile Motel, because the sign outside said it had a heated pool.

20. CANNONBALL

The left wall, the one against which the cheap, prefabricated headboards of the two queen-sized beds have been pushed, is a floor-to-ceiling mural of a tropical sunset. I sit in the room's only chair, facing the sunset, my back to the television set, which leaks sound and colour into the motel room. My children have each claimed a bed for themselves and they leap from one to the other, each invading their sibling's realm as they fight for control of the remote. When one of them gains a strong enough grip on it, they flick to the show of their choice until, seconds later, the other wrestles it away, aims at the television, and changes the channel.

I stare at the sunset. Or maybe it's a sunrise? I decide that it's definitely a sunset. Although the code of sibling conduct prevents them from voicing their curiosity, they both wonder why I haven't intervened, re-established order by decreeing some time limitation on the remote, ten minutes for you, then ten minutes for you. They continue fighting and bickering as they wait for me to provide justice. When I don't do this, their sense of safety begins wiggling away, like the last tiny strands holding a loose tooth in place. The absence of parental authority makes them fight harder for the remote control, but the louder they get, the more urgency they use to defend their perspective of fair, the more effectively I'm able to tune them out. I sit motionless, staring at the sunset until I hear a clumsy crash and Jenny screaming as she loses her balance and falls into the space between the bed and the wall. Her body hits the floor with a snap-sudden thud. Jack freezes, stands motionless on the bed with his pillow-holding arms locked at the end of his swing. A cartoon explosion fills the room. The sound of an eighteen-wheeler on the highway gets louder and then fades away. Finally, Jenny's head, unbloodied and unbroken, pokes up beside the bed.

"Not fair!" she says. "Not fair!"

"Get changed! We're going swimming!" I yell, masking my fear with anger. I look back at the sunset. A second later, I glance to the right and see that my kids are standing there, wearing their bathing suits. I have no idea how long they've been there like that, with their naked toes curled into the short brown carpet.

"Are you okay?" Jack asks me.

"I'm fine. Good. Great."

"Did you bring towels?"

"Towels?"

"For swimming..."

"Right."

"Did you bring any?"

"Aren't there towels in the bathroom?"

"You go check," Jack tells Jenny.

She does not protest. Walking with her weight on her toes, as if she were crossing a short distance of hot sand, Jenny makes her way to the bathroom. For a reason that will never become known to me, she flushes the toilet.

On the TV, a man jumps out of a plane. He looks directly into the camera as he pulls the ripcord. Jack notices me staring at the screen. He turns off the television as Jenny returns from the bathroom. She has a thin, bleached-white towel around her neck. There's another towel in her right hand. Several small square washcloths are tucked under her arm. Jack surveys Jenny's discoveries and is unimpressed.

"There were tons of towels in there!" One of the washcloths underneath Jenny's arm falls onto the carpet.

"Mom would have remembered to bring beach towels," Jack says. I don't correct him. For the first time since entering room 9, I get up from the chair. Opening the door, I squint into the suddenly stunning sunlight, and the kids follow me outside.

The pool is empty, but three people sit around it. A couple in their early sixties have claimed the midpoint on the far side of the rectangular pool. The dyed-blond wife wears a navy blue one-piece and flips through a glossy magazine, flicking the pages like every visual depicted strikes her as a personal insult. To her right, her husband talks into an out-of-date cellphone, the kind that looks like a communicator from the first *Star Trek* series. He speaks with a stern voice, barking orders to an employee as the grey hairs on his stomach climb his beer gut like sherpas. Both the husband and the wife appear to be sincerely attempting to enjoy this one last warm day, an endeavour they are evidently failing at to an equal degree, which makes them perfect for each other.

At the far end of the pool is a fifty-year-old woman wearing a red bikini. Her midriff is thirty years too young for her. Her skin is tanned. Her hands are wrinkled and ringless. The lounger in which she lounges is perfectly perpendicular to the black sans-serif letters that spell out DEEP END. The black circular sunglasses hiding her eyes create the impression of a wannabe starlet, possibly from the late seventies, someone who's spent the last thirty years right here, at this pool, waiting to be discovered. She smiles as the three of us enter the pool area, while the couple of a certain age have rendered us invisible, so I sit closer to her, kicking a lounger with my foot to angle it into the sun.

The white plastic looks dirty but it isn't, just stained by dust over time, but the blue webbing sags as I sit, so I don't lie down, choosing instead to perch on the edge of it and put the majority of my weight on my knees. When I look around for my kids, I find them in the air, their arms wrapped around their legs, having already leapt from the black-and-white-tiled edge of the pool, hovering three feet above the calm flat surface of the water, both of them mid-cannonball. Never before has time moved as slowly for me as it does in this moment. The sun is a performer stepping through the velvet curtains of a puffy white cloud. The wind is soft and warm. The surface of the water looks like Jell-O wrapped in cellophane. There is no fear, not even aware-ness that fear exists, in the faces of my children. Every inch of their skin, of the muscles beneath it, of the very bone structure contributed by me, my wife, and the count-less generations that came before us is being employed to express nothing but this pure absolute joy. It is as if all evolution, the entire history of life here on earth, has been nothing but an orchestrated sequence of events allowing this moment, this articulation of fun and freedom.

Whatever trancelike state I've gotten myself into allows me to continue stretching this moment. Jenny and Jack float in the air and only after a significant amount of time do they begin descending toward the water, moving in tiny increments toward a future they do not fear. Know-ing, without doubt, that victory is theirs. And somehow, because I'm seeing this, because they're mine, that victory belongs to me as well. I watch them fall, frame by frame, their excitement increasing as they near the surface. When my children finally hit it, they produce an impressive splash, and I feel something inside of me change, like stubborn fingers finally letting go of something that didn't belong to them in the first place.

Their heads fully submerge. There is a moment when the diminishing waves produced by the splash are the only movement in the world. Then they both break the surface, regular speed, proving that the spell is already broken.

In the absence of pool toys, Jenny and Jack splash each other with their hands. The older couple, perhaps looking for a reason to leave, perhaps sincerely annoyed, pack up their belongings and storm unhappily away. The kids don't notice, and I don't care. I let the kids make all the noise they want. I encourage them to do so, occasionally redirecting them when their play gets too rough. I lose track of time. I'm unable to date the last occasion when I've simply watched them play.

The sun has started to set when the Wannabe Starlet packs up her things. She pulls off her dark sunglasses as she walks past me. Her eyes are green and clear and project the kind of wisdom I've always longed to be judged by. She puts her hand on my shoulder.

"You're a good father," she says. She walks away. I pretend to wipe sweat from my forehead and cry into the white towel as silently as I can. They don't swim for much longer, maybe ten or fifteen more minutes, and then we mutually agree to go, having found everything we came for.

The kids are back in their street clothes, their wet hair staining the white pillows as they watch television, their bodies and spirits calmed by swimming. I lock myself in the bathroom. I call Julie. It goes directly to voice mail. I immediately call her back, and she answers on the first ring.

"Hello?" Her voice is full of concern.

"I've got the kids."

"Okay?"

169

"I'm going to take them to a movie. And supper, too. We'll be home later. You'll have the house to yourself."

"That'll be nice."

"Julie?"

"Yes?"

There is a pause, which gets harder to break the longer I wait, a crack growing into a jump, a leap. I don't have much time. I must speak now or forever hold my peace.

"I miss you. I really miss you."

"I miss you, too."

I can hear her fingers continuing to type. It is a moment that could have easily provoked me, which I could interpret as a lack of respect, one more piece of evidence that she takes me for granted. But right now, in this moment, her distraction, the routineness it generates, seems like a miracle.

"Okay."

"Have fun. Say hi to the kids for me."

I hang up the phone. I place the room key on the middle of the still-made bed and marshal the kids into the car. The engine is running when I see that Jenny has failed to close the door behind her. It is with the intention of closing it that I leave the keys swinging in the ignition and head back to the room. The doorknob is in my hand but I fail to stop there, continuing back into room 9. I nod at the tropical sunset, greeting it like an old friend. I look at my feet on the thin brown carpet. In the bathroom, I find a miniature cake of soap wrapped in thick, smooth paper. I remove this wrapping. The soap has been given the scent of coconut. I push one corner of the denuded bar into the palm of my right hand. The other corner I press against the mirror. Using thick block capitals, I write what I have learned:

THERE IS NO LEAVING THIS PLACE.
YOU WILL ALWAYS BE HERE.
THE BEST YOU CAN DO IS ENJOY
WHAT YOU HAVE.

I set down the soap. I wash my hands. I use a thin white towel to dry them. I leave the motel room door open as I exit. The kids are silent as they sit in the back seat of the car. The motor idles. When I turn on the radio, they both start breathing again. A pop song we all know the words to comes on. I am already turning up the volume when both Jenny and Jack ask me to do so. We leave the parking lot. We get back on the highway, heading east, toward the city.

ACKNOWLEDGEMENTS

The author wishes to reinterate that this is a work of fiction and thank the following people without whose support this book would never have been completed: Marlo Miazga, Christopher Frey, Stephanie Domet, Zach Picard, Sheila Heti, Sam Hyate, Kelvin Kong, Carl Knudson, Mike Volpe, Peter Atto, Scott Pack, Phoenix, Frida, Karen and Barry, Liz, Rolly and Shirley, Leigh, Megan, Andrew, and everyone at Invisible, the Canada Council for the Arts, the Superior Court of Justice, and the staff of the Toronto City Hall Wedding Chapel.

INVISIBLE PUBLISHING is a not-for-profit publishing company that produces contemporary works of fiction, creative non-fiction, and poetry. We're small in scale, but we take our work, and our mission, seriously: we publish material that's engaging, literary, current, and uniquely Canadian.

We are committed to publishing diverse voices and experiences. In acknowledging historical and systemic barriers, and the limits of our existing catalogue, we strongly encourage Indigenous and writers of colour to submit their work.

Invisible Publishing is also home to the Bibliophonic series, and the Snare and Throwback imprints.

If you'd like to know more please get in touch:
info@invisiblepublishing.com

Invisible Publishing
Halifax & Picton